TILLA

By Ilse Koehn

MISCHLING, SECOND DEGREE:
My Childhood in Nazi Germany

TILLA

ILSE KOEHN
Tilla

GREENWILLOW BOOKS
New York

Printed in the United States of America
First Edition   10 9 8 7 6 5 4 3 2 1

Library of Congress Cataloging in Publication Data
Koehn, Ilse.   Tilla.
Summary: The lives of two teenagers become
increasingly entwined as they pursue their few
surviving dreams in post-World War II Berlin.
[1. World War, 1939-1945—Germany—Fiction.
2. Germany—History—Allied occupation,
1945- —Fiction]   I. Title.
PZ7.K8178Ti   [Fic]   81-2217
ISBN 0-688-00650-7   AACR2

To JOHN
and KYLE

PROLOGUE

Franklin D. Roosevelt, President of the United States of America, was seated in the center. He didn't smile. On his left, his face inscrutable, sat British Prime Minister Winston Churchill. On the right, Soviet Marshal Joseph Stalin seemed the most relaxed, least solemn of these three powerful men.

Behind them stood their foreign ministers and secretaries. As flashbulbs went off, only Vyacheslav Molotov, the Soviet foreign commissar, and British Undersecretary Sir Alexander Cadogan looked directly into the cameras. The moment was recorded:

FEBRUARY 4–11, 1945

YALTA

Crimea, USSR

THREE-POWER CONFERENCE

Though the war was still being fought, victory for the Allies was in sight. The three leaders had come together to formulate their postwar policies. What to do with Germany after its certain defeat had been the most urgent problem.

They had agreed to divide it into four separate zones of occupation. The Soviet Union had agreed to a French zone only on the condition that it be carved out of the territories allotted to the United States and Britain.

The German capital, Berlin, would be given a special status. As a symbol of the Grand Alliance that won the war, the Four Powers would occupy and rule it jointly.

The city itself, like the country as a whole, would be divided into four sectors, each sector governed by one of the Four Powers. The administration of Berlin would be vested in a *Kommandatura* made up of the military heads of the forces of the Four Powers.

Roosevelt, Churchill, and Stalin agreed to meet again in a few months, after the victory. Until then there would be a concerted Anglo-American effort in Italy and on the western front as well as massive air strikes on Germany so that it would not be able to transfer forces to the east, where the Russians were about to launch their final big offensive.

PART ONE

1

"Let her sleep! Nothing's going to happen here."

"But, Mother! Listen! My God! Listen to all those planes! There must be thousands."

"Stop worrying, Adele," Mother Westfal said to her daughter. "They're not going to waste their bombs on the fields and woods around here. They're probably on the way to Berlin again."

The two women looked at the sleeping girl under the big down comforter.

"How tired she was," said Adele, "coming all the way from Dresden. Thirty miles on a bike in a day! That's a lot for a fifteen-year-old."

"It'll give her strong legs," said her mother, "and don't forget, she's getting twenty pounds of potatoes to take home.

Nowadays people *walk* that distance to get potatoes. Come to think of it, maybe fifteen would be enough?"

"Fifteen? Mother! You got six plates of the finest Meissen china for . . . a few pounds of potatoes. Twenty pounds is nothing. Do you know what those plates are worth?"

The old woman shrugged. "Same as all other fancy things now—nothing. You can't eat 'em. We have food because we work hard. Our small farm has provided for us. But it sure hasn't come easy. Your fancy friends come begging now, like her mother. They don't like to get their hands dirty." She nodded toward the sleeping girl.

"That's not fair!" Adele replied angrily. "Lisa Wenkenberg isn't like that."

"She could have planted a garden or come out here to help, no? But she's too good for that. She'd rather send her little girl thirty miles on a bike—in *these* times! *Ach!*"

The vibrations of the heavy motors of hundreds and hundreds of bombers shook the farmhouse, made the glass in the cupboard and the Meissen plates tinkle. Both women stared at the ceiling, their faces solemn.

The radio, on very low, crackled with static, and the soft music was suddenly interrupted by the announcer's voice: "Attention! Attention! Attention! An attack is coming! Go to your cellars at once! Repeat, at once!"

It was 10:10 P.M. on Tuesday, February 13, 1945. The beginning of Lent, the eve of Ash Wednesday, and Operation Thunderclap was under way.

Thunderclap was the Allied code name for a series of

large-scale bombing raids designed to deliver the final blows to German morale. The first target was the city of Dresden, and everything was going according to plan.

Six minutes earlier, at exactly 10:04 P.M., two squadrons of Lancaster bombers had reached Dresden and dropped parachute flares to mark the general position of the city. Planes of the Mosquito type had followed to identify specific targets with red indicator bombs. Now Plate Rack, the call name of the main force of bombers, was on its way to make the actual strike.

At 10:15, right on schedule, the Plate Rack force started dumping its deadly load. A rain of high-explosive bombs came down on the city, followed by incendiaries, which burned what had not been smashed.

It took only six minutes to destroy the Old Town section of Dresden. At 10:21 P.M. it was engulfed in flames, allowing the master bomber to relay a message back to England that the target had been successfully attacked.

Dresden shook as if from an earthquake. Fire joined fire, heating the air to more than 1,000 degrees Fahrenheit, generating a fire storm of indescribable terror.

When their house became a blazing furnace, Lisa Wenkenberg and her seven-year-old son, Rudi, had tried to escape but, like leaves, had been sucked back into the fire. Nothing remained of them when the second wave of 529 Lancaster bombers arrived at 1:23 A.M. They dropped masses of the big blockbuster bombs and 650,000 incendiaries, making the inferno below even more hellish. But it was not over.

A few hours later the third and last wave came. Now 450 American Flying Fortresses, escorted by 288 P-51 Mustangs, finished the destruction of the city.

How many people perished is unknown. How many died from direct hits by bombs or debris, how many were suffocated by carbon monoxide in shelters, and how many were literally roasted to death, no one will ever know. Official estimates vary between 30,000 and 200,000 killed.

Dresden was destroyed. The sixteenth-century capital of the province of Saxony with its fairy-tale spires and cobblestone streets, with some of the most beautiful examples of Baroque architecture in the world, was reduced to 1,600 square acres of rubble.

2 She had made it and brought home twenty pounds of potatoes. Mama would be pleased that she had remembered to wrap them into newspapers so that they would not freeze. And the three onions would make her happy, Renate thought. Adele had quickly, furtively dropped them into her bag, so that the old woman wouldn't notice. And when she shook her hand to say good-bye, there had been an apple in it. A small, slightly shriveled apple, but an apple nevertheless. She had had to tear herself from the wailing Adele, who had tried to keep her from going and didn't seem to understand that she had

to get back home, that her mother was waiting.

Renate stood leaning on her bike, and looking at the pile of still-smoldering rubble, she did not, could not comprehend that her home and her street simply were no longer there.

She watched a group of Hitler Youth boys, in morbid fascination, as they stacked up corpses. Sometimes an arm or leg would just fall off, and they'd pick it up, like a part of a doll, and fling it on top of the pile.

"Renatken!"

Startled, she turned, looked at . . . was that Mr. Breuer? The man who had the newsstand on the corner? Had had, for there was neither corner nor newsstand left.

"Renatken!" he called again in a hoarse and high-pitched voice. His face was black, so were his clothes. They hung on him like rags, burned, scorched rags. His hair and eyebrows were burned off. A wave of the sickening, sweet smell of burned flesh preceded him. She shrank back when he stretched his arms out, as if to embrace her. His eyes glistened strangely: the eyes of a madman.

"Renatken! Come here, Renatken!"

She moved behind her bike.

"Don't like Uncle Breuer anymore, ha?" And then he suddenly started to laugh, almost doubled over with hysterical, spine-chilling laughter, and intoned in a singsong voice, "Roasted, roasted. They were all roasted like Easter lambs. Every single one of them. My Clara and little Trudy, the Schillers and old Marta Schwindt and Lisa Wenkenberg with that little rascal, Rudi. All dead, all roasted like Easter lambs." He bent backward, laughing again, laughing crazily.

Renate grabbed her bike and ran, ran, stumbled, fell, and got up. She ran from that high-pitched insane voice repeating, "ALL ROASTED—ALL DEAD."

She would never remember where she had been and how long she had walked and stumbled through the rubble of her hometown, the potato bag banging against the front wheel of her bike. But she would remember the stench, the sweet, nauseating stench that had been everywhere, and the bodies. Hundreds of bodies in the shallow pond in Altmarkt Park. Piles of bodies being burned with flamethrowers. Bodies being stacked along the wall of the burned and bombed-out railroad station. Bodies of people and animals covering the lawns of the zoo. She'd remember the leopard grotesquely hanging in a tree. Clothed corpses and naked corpses and pieces of corpses floating in the Elbe River, as she crossed the Augustus Bridge along with a stream of survivors. A crowd in trance that staggered away from disaster. Ghastly apparitions with blackened faces, dead eyes, and burned clothing. Some dragged along remnants of their possessions in handcarts. Others carried suitcases or clutched objects. One woman was pushing a baby carriage, and in it was only the blackened, scorched corpse of her child.

Once they reached the *Autobahn*, the main highway, the crowd, as if by silent agreement, turned west. West, away from the approaching Russian army. Renate turned north.

3 "Attention! Attention! This is Radio Berlin! Enemy planes have just passed Hamburg and are continuing on an east-southeast course. An attack on the German capital has to be expected."

At Schlosstrasse 7, a three-story apartment house in the Berlin suburb of Hermsdorf, Elizabeth Hoffart thought, *Here we go again*, and turned off her radio.

A tall woman, forty-two years of age, she had the flawless complexion, large, round eyes, and small, heart-shaped mouth of a china doll—and usually the same, fixed smile. She had a good figure, slim in the waist and round in the hips. Her most outstanding feature, however, was a bosom of truly imposing size, which was not necessarily a manifestation of a loving and generous nature.

She went to the balcony door and made sure it was ajar, then closed the heavy drapes over all the windows, pulling one drape over the other so that they overlapped and fastening them there with safety pins. This, she hoped, would prevent glass from flying all over the place, in case bombs fell close by and the windows broke.

She was proud of her comfortable apartment, especially of the balcony room, as she liked to call the living room. In addition, she had a bedroom and a dressing room. They were small and narrow. One contained her bed, a chair, and a nightstand, and the other an old wooden wardrobe and dresser. Nothing else could possibly fit in. She also had a kitchen and bath, which were always spick-and-span.

The widow Hoffart, born Wenkenberg, was orderly. Everything but dirt had its place. That, she thought, was one of the few advantages of living alone. Not that Albert, bless his soul, had been messy. She sighed. Already eleven years had passed since he had died suddenly of a heart attack, after only two years of marriage. Well, if it hadn't been that, he might have died in the war, like her brother, Erwin. Erwin and now Lisa and the children, the only relatives she had had. After what she had heard about the Dresden air raid, she was sure that they were dead.

Outside, the sirens started howling. She looked in the mirror, combed her short brown hair, dabbed just a touch of rouge on her cheeks, then put on her coat. "What a way to prepare for the night," she said out loud, and picked up her small suitcase and purse. She switched off the light and went downstairs to join the other tenants in the air-raid shelter, which was the cellar.

4 February is a bleak month. February 1945 in Germany did not even hold the joyous promise of spring. Spring, yes, but no joy, only the certain prospect of defeat for the nation. The war was being fought on German soil, and the country was being battered from the air day and night. Food, clothing, and just about everything else, including coal to heat homes, were scarce or

nonexistent. Few doubted that the end of the war and defeat were imminent. It was only a question of when and how. How to survive was foremost in everyone's mind. Many thought that their chances were best in the west, West Germany, where the American, British, and French armies would be. So they moved west by any means available. The homeless and those who lived in the path of the Russian army—they all pushed west.

Coming out of Dresden, Renate had been swept along with the crowd. Now she was going against it. It came toward her, as far as she could see. The trucks came, and the horse-drawn wagons and cars. They were packed and piled high with refugees and their belongings, loaded to a point where the vehicles below often were almost invisible. In between were those who rode bikes and mothers walking hand in hand with their children. Everyone who walked seemed to drag or push a cart, baby carriage, or some home-built contraption on wheels. These, too, were laden with boxes and blankets, pots and pans, items of every imaginable kind. And intermittently there were the trucks, tanks, and guns of the German army and groups of German soldiers on foot, Red Cross convoys with the wounded, and occasionally soldiers on motorcycles. They filled the road from one side to the other, spilled over onto the shoulder, the ditches, the fields, flooding west—away from the Russians.

Renate, small and skinny for her age, resolutely walked her bike through the crowd, dodging as many pushes and shoves as possible. There was but one thought in her mind:

I have to get to my aunt. I have to get to Aunt Liz. "Mrs. Elizabeth Hoffart. Berlin-Hermsdorf, Schlosstrasse Seven," she muttered to herself over and over again, afraid that she would forget the address if she stopped.

Suddenly there were two small children in front of her. She turned sharply left, trying to avoid them and, as she did, was hit by something strapped to the outside of a car. She was thrown over onto her bike and screamed when the unconcerned crowd kept on walking, stepping on her as if she were nothing but an old rag on the road.

The scream made the crowd nearest her pause, giving her time and room to get up. She hurt, but nothing seemed broken, so she pushed and scrambled her way to the side of the road and out into a soggy field and up a hill until she found herself under a big old oak tree—and suddenly quite alone.

5 Emil Troester pulled the cap down over his ears and turned up the collar of his coat. "Miserable weather, as miserable as the times," he muttered as he stepped out into the cold drizzle and walked down the brick path toward the garden gate. He had made that path, laid the bricks himself, cemented them in properly. Done it right. Slowly, thoughtfully, and carefully—the way he did everything, just as his dad had taught him. *That's*

why they're still in place, he thought, *every single one of them—after God knows how many years.* He had been young then. Twenty-four or -five, and they had just moved in, he and Trude. Ah! What's the use of thinking about the past?

Time to take a walk, see for himself that there were so many refugees that traffic on the *Autobahn* was creeping along at a snail's pace. He also needed to get away from the house for a while. Too much noise. *You've lived alone too long, you old codger*, he chided himself. *Not used to little kids anymore. Too many people for my small house.*

It would have been easier if he hadn't allowed the old couple to stay. But they had been so utterly miserable, nowhere to sleep, nowhere to go, how could he, an old man, living all alone, have refused them? He couldn't complain about them. They had nestled themselves into the cellar, stayed there almost the whole time—quiet as mice.

But now there were Anna and Gerda, too, *and* Gerda's three children, the youngest only three months old. So he slept on the living-room couch, while they had the bedroom. Too small even that. Too little of everything. Not enough blankets, pillows, towels, not enough of anything. Too little for too many. He'd have to build some kinds of cots for the two little boys; they shouldn't sleep on the floor. Anyway, he never could have turned away his only sister, her daughter, and the children. *They have, at least, a roof over their heads. God knows how long we'll be able to keep it.*

He walked through the drizzle and the dripping woods, then climbed the hill from which he could see the main road.

13

Hitler's, the Fuehrer's, *Autobahn*. There it was, the dismal sight of the homeless. Thousands and thousands. It was more than he cared to see. He had turned to go back home when something caught his eye. Under the big oak lay a small, wet heap of utter misery. She cowered under her bicycle, which shook in rhythm with her sobs. He coughed. Nothing. He coughed again, waited, and finally said, "I'm Emil Troester. And who are you?"

It came muffled and monotone, an automatic answer to an ordinary question: "Renate Wenkenberg. Dresden, Rathausstrasse Ten A."

He barely suppressed the shocked exclamation. Dresden. *—Dear God! There is no such thing as a Rathausstrasse in Dresden anymore* . . . stood there desperately trying to find the right words. Haltingly, as gently as possible he asked, "Your people, Renate? Is there . . . Do you have anyone left?"

The wet little head with the tangled pigtails nodded, but it seemed an eternity before she answered between sobs, "My aunt. I have an aunt in Berlin. Her name is Mrs. Elizabeth Hoffart and she lives Berlin-Hermsdorf, Schlosstrasse Seven. I have to get to my aunt!" She was suddenly on her feet, looked at him with extraordinary large gray eyes in her pale, tearstained face.

He guessed that she was about fourteen or fifteen years old. A small, skinny kid with a muddy coat, long, muddy pants, and the left pants leg torn at the knee. The red scarf, which had caught his attention, had slipped completely off her head. He pulled it back on gingerly.

"If it hadn't been for this scarf, Renate, I would never have seen you. Little Red Riding Hood. Come along with me, so we can get you dry, get something hot into you and—"

"I have to get to Berlin!"

"You won't be alone with me! My sister's there, and her daughter and her three children, and an old couple. Full house! You'll be as safe with us as anyone can be nowadays."

"But I have to get to my aunt!"

"After you've had a night's rest, Renate. Tomorrow."

"But!"

"No buts. It's getting dark and the road is no place for a young girl at night. You know what's going on down there!" When she nodded and he saw that she was ready to cry again, he quickly went on. "I promise you, you can leave as early tomorrow as you wish. As soon as there's daylight. I have a hunch that you're a very tired girl and a hungry one. When was the last time you had anything to eat?"

There was a long pause. He could hardly hear her when she finally answered, "I don't know." She looked at him, bent her head, and shuffled her feet before she continued in a very different, much stronger voice: "But I have some potatoes here." She pointed to the dirty, battered bag, which seemed to be filled with old newspapers. "I mean . . . I can pay you. Not with money," she added quickly, "but if you let me stay tonight, I can give you the potatoes. I have twenty pounds!" And when he didn't instantly respond, she said, "And three onions."

15

He smiled to reassure her. "Child, you can't pay me for what any decent person should do! Don't you know that twenty pounds of potatoes can get you a room at the Ritz? That's the finest hotel there is! What I have to offer you is worth only three potatoes."

She nodded solemnly and stuck out her hand.

"You want to shake hands on it? Fine." His warm, bony old man's hand closed around hers, and he was surprised that that small, cold hand had such a firm grip.

They walked hand in hand, he pushing her bike, trying to make small talk, while he wondered how to dry her things, where to have her sleep, and how to cover her.

6 They all were gathered around the living-room table. Gerda, the baby in her lap, sat next to Renate. The two small boys were in between Gerda and the old couple. Emil Troester and his sister stood, old Anna leaning on the table and her brother.

"Forty-seven, forty-eight, forty-nine, fifty! Fifty-one, fifty-two, fifty-three." It was almost a moan, and "fifty-four" became a unanimous sigh. Eight very different voices pronouncing in awe "fifty-four."

On the table, being counted, lay Renate's potatoes. Each one an entity with its own space around it, they were neatly arranged in rows. Five rows of ten and one short row of four potatoes were being appraised and judged by eight pairs of eyes, as if they were precious jewels.

"Child!" old Anna said in her hoarse voice. "You got cheated, child! That's no twenty pounds! Sixteen maybe, more likely fifteen."

"And this one—and that—and . . . FIVE are rotten!" one of the little boys shouted, and his brother, pointing an accusing finger, added triumphantly, "And three are kind of smashed."

"Those are mine," said Emil Troester, and quickly picked them up. "Renate and I have a deal," he said over Gerda's and Anna's protests, "and a deal is a deal."

"But you should take good ones," objected Renate.

"That wasn't in the deal! Red Riding Hood, I can choose any I want, and I want the smashed ones. They'll go nicely into our big soup pot. You'll feel all right eating with us, and no one here will feel that they are not getting a fair share." He quickly lifted both his hands to stop protests from all corners. "No arguments, please. This is my house— and that's how I want it. *Basta*. Boys! Get me some newspapers from the kitchen. We'll wrap up the rest of the potatoes again, so Renate has something to bring to her aunt."

"The rotten ones, too?" one of the boys asked.

It was old Anna who answered, "No. Take them to the kitchen. I'll bet there are some usable parts on them still."

The only source of heat in the house, aside from the coal-burning kitchen stove, was a big old tile oven in the corner of the living room. There Renate's boots, stuffed with newspapers, stood drying. Draped over it were her coat, long

17

pants, and stockings. Renate, wrapped in a blanket, sat with her back against it, unable to keep her eyes open, unable to stay awake. It was all a dream. A strange dream. Thousands of faces, unfamiliar faces coming toward her, and cars and tanks. Her head fell forward. The movement woke her up, and she found herself looking into old Anna's eyes. Heard Anna say something about sleep, felt a soft pillow behind her head—and then everything was warm. Warm and comfortable and good. Mama was in the kitchen, and Rudi, as usual, up to mischief. She could hear Mama laugh softly and Rudi giggle. There was also a man's voice. Mama was talking to someone else. Papa. Papa was home. She heard him say, "Don't wake her up," because there was that noise again, and she was frightened. But he said again, "Don't wake her up. They're not coming here." She suddenly knew what the noise was: planes, enemy planes. But Papa said there was nothing to worry about. They were going someplace else. "They'll never bomb Dresden, because it's too beautiful. They know it, have to admit it, the English and the Americans, even the Russians. They'll never hurt Dresden." Mama and Papa kept on talking softly in the kitchen, and the noise had stopped, so everything was all right. She could go on sleeping. She felt warm and cozy and awfully tired. There was the familiar clatter of dishes and, best of all, the smell of dinner.

She opened her eyes when she heard her name, saw soup and bread, ate as if in a dream. Her mind just refused to wake up. She was dimly aware of great commotion, furniture being moved, and talk. A lot of talk about curtains. Why curtains?

Suddenly she stood alone in a small, tidy kitchen and did not know where she was or how she had gotten there. There was a towel over her arm and a cake of soap in her hand. Whose kitchen, towel, soap? Her mind refused to figure it out. In the center of the kitchen sat a big tin tub, filled with hot water, which was inviting, and she knew it was for her. She washed and dried herself. But how to clean up? You always have to clean up. Mama was very strict about it. You always have to clean up, especially if you're in someone else's house. But how to get the water out of the tub and into the sink? She looked around for a pitcher, a bowl, anything, and then remembered only that someone had taken her by the arm, wrapped her up as if she were a little kid, and then she was snuggled into something funny-smelling. But it was cozy and warm, and she had fallen asleep.

She woke up slowly, saw big red and yellow flowers all around her, and realized suddenly that the flowers belonged to Mr. Troester's living-room curtains, that she had been sleeping on them, in them. Her bed was two easy chairs with a stool between them.

Suddenly she knew where she was and why and did not want to know, would have liked to crawl back into the flowers, bury herself in them. Not to know! Oh, not to have to think.

When she became aware of Mr. Troester's concerned face, she tried to suppress the tears, tried bravely to smile.

"Did you sleep all right? Were you warm enough, Renate, in the little dreamboat we made you?"

She managed, "Thank you. Yes," and the rest came out

by itself: "Oh, I wish I could stay here forever!" It was a wail she couldn't help. Crying, she buried her head into the flowers of the curtains.

"You can! Renate? Renate! Listen! Listen!" He patted her head. "We want you to stay. Please, child, we all want you with us."

She liked him, trusted him. Yes, if he were her grandpa . . . the thought had given her another crying fit because she had never even had a grandpa, never known her grandparents. *But I do have Aunt Liz.* Her head kept repeating it. *I do have a real aunt, and that's where I belong.* Her mind was made up. She had to refuse, refuse as politely as she knew how. Mr. Troester seemed to understand. In a way that made her feel worse, made her want to stay more than she cared to admit. But there was no choice. She couldn't become a burden to Mr. Troester, who, after all, was a stranger, as long as she had someone of her own family. She had to get to her aunt. That's where she belonged.

7 The day was cold and gray and windy. Big clouds were scudding over the sky, but at least it wasn't raining. Renate pedaled steadily. Schwarzheide, Schlippkau, Klettwitz. BERLIN/100 miles; BERLIN/90 miles. She was not interested in the names of the villages she passed, only in the road signs that told her the mileage

to Berlin. Berlin, that's where she wanted to be. Home with Aunt Liz.

Now she was glad that she hadn't stayed with Mr. Troester. Once they knew that nothing could change her mind, Gerda had looked much happier and old Anna was clearly relieved. She thought of a sentence she had heard often lately: Who needs another mouth to feed in these times? No one, of course. No one needed a stranger, but an aunt, that was something else. Mr. Troester, though, she knew, had been genuinely sad to see her go.

She touched the shoulder strap of the small canvas bag he had given her. He said that he had worn it all through the First World War, and that was twenty-seven years ago. She loved the bag, had been quick to put her shriveled apple and the three onions into it. He had added a shallow tin bowl and a tin fork, spoon, and knife. And as if this weren't enough, he had also given her a worn-out money purse for the two-mark-fifty her mother had given her, which she had carried loose in her coat pocket, and then he had handed her a ten-mark bill. That, he said, was for a room in a hotel or pension, and she had to promise not to be on the road at night. "If they want more money," he advised, "give them some of your potatoes."

Forty-six potatoes. I have forty-six potatoes left, and three onions, one shriveled apple, and *twelve-mark-fifty. I am rich and only eighty-five miles to Berlin now.*

Though there were many refugees even on the side roads, riding her bike was no problem, not like yesterday's nightmare. She was making good progress. So good that she had started looking for a barn, someplace where she could be out of the wind and rest for a while, when a ragged-looking soldier barred her way and shouted, "*Halt!,*" then demanded in a quiet but menacing way, "Give me that bike!"

"No!" she said. "*No!* This is my bike. I need it. I have to get to my aunt!"

He grabbed the handlebar, started pulling, tried to wrench it away from her, but Renate held on with all her might, screaming, "It's my bike! I need it! Help! Please help!" The stream of refugees flowed past, and no one even so much as looked. How could all those people pass and ignore her cries for help, ignore the fact that this soldier was trying to steal her bike? She wanted to clutch at the people passing by; but they moved away out of reach, and he was so much stronger she didn't know how long she'd be able to hold on. He had the handlebars firmly in his grip, and she had only a hold on the seat. She screamed louder, and then he suddenly kicked her—a vicious kick of such force against her shin that she reeled backward. As she fell, she saw him mount her bike.

She was lying on the road when she came to, and the first thing she saw was one shiny black boot. Then she saw the other and behind it a wheel that obviously belonged to a motorcycle.

"You all right?" a man's voice asked. The owner of the voice, it turned out, was also the owner of the boots. He was a young officer, and with him were two others. She sat up, then got up without any trouble, though her head and leg hurt. The three officers and their heavy BMWs were standing in a triangle, in the center of which was her bike and the soldier who had tried to steal it.

"I'm all right, I think," said Renate, but no one was interested in her answer—or her. The three officers were facing the soldier, who looked pale, pitiful in his torn, dirty uniform, especially in contrast with the immaculate black uniforms of the others.

It was the oldest of the three officers who spoke, and his voice was like a whip. "So you lost your unit?" He looked at the tattered document in his hand, tore it up, and threw the pieces toward the soldier. "That's what this is worth!" he scoffed as the wind blew the pieces right back at him. He did not seem to notice, for he went on, "As far as I'm concerned, you have no papers. A soldier without papers is AWOL—in other words, you are a deserter! Deserters are to be shot on the spot. You know that, don't you?"

The soldier began to shake and stammer. He gesticulated desperately, as if his hands could convey the words he was unable to utter. The officer with the menacing voice turned in disgust and saw Renate. Without getting off his motorcycle, he moved just enough to allow a small passage into the triangle.

"Get your bike, girl, and take off," he commanded.

Renate hesitated.

"You are all right, aren't you?"

"Yes, I think so."

"Then take that bike and move on!"

"Yes, sir!" she said timidly, and reached for it.

"That's better. Get going—get-get-get, girl. This is no

23

time to dawdle. There's a war on. Don't you know?"

She took her bike then, got on, got away, pedaled as fast as she could.

8 ". . . and? Did they shoot him?"

"I don't know," said Renate.

"I would have stayed to find out."

"No! You wouldn't have," she replied angrily, "not if an officer told you to move. You would have moved, too!"

"Maybe," said the boy, and grinned.

He was almost sixteen, he said, no taller than Renate and equally skinny. He had short, very fine blond hair, big brown eyes, and dimples. He wore the Hitler Youth uniform, and his name was Rolf.

After getting her bicycle back, she had ridden a long time and finally spotted a barn just when she thought she could go no farther. It wasn't really a barn, more a shed, since one side was completely open. But it was full of hay.

Hoping that no one would notice and stop her, she had walked toward it, found a slightly open door on the side, and slid in. A resounding "BOO" had made her jump and almost frightened her out of her skull.

It had been Rolf, who had emerged, laughing, from the hay. She didn't think it very funny. Still breathless, she told him of her experiences.

He said, "Maybe you should have given him your bike?"

24

She wasn't sure whether he was kidding or not. He added, "I think they shot him, don't you?"

"Stop it!" Renate demanded. "I don't want to hear about it anymore."

"Do you think they'll shoot me?" he persisted.

"Why should they shoot you? You are not a deserter!"

"I am, in a way. Fuehrer's order, as you know. No one leaves his post of duty. If you do, you're a deserter and will be shot on the spot."

"Your post of duty? You're too young. Where do you think your post of duty is? Where do you think you should be?"

"Lomnitz," came his reply as he started playing with a few strands of hay. "Except the Russians are already there. You see, I was with my school in one of those stupid evacuation camps. Camp!" he snorted. "It was a pretty fancy hotel, let me tell you. Nothing but the best for Betzi. Our director and Latin and Greek teacher, Mr. Dr. Berthold Betz. Every day the front was coming closer, until we could differentiate among the sounds of grenade launchers, flame-throwers, even rifle shots—and no one knew what to do. Betzi was waiting for relocation orders, but they never arrived. That guy was supposed to be in charge. In charge! He had his pants full. You know what he did? He and our two other teachers? They packed their car and disappeared during the night. Made themselves scarce, as the saying goes. Took off to the tune of 'Let the devil take the hindmost.' We, Germany's youth and future . . . ? He didn't give a shit.

"Anyway, Fred and Eddy, our Hitler Youth leaders,

made us pack our knapsacks in a hurry. Just in time, because the Russians arrived only two hours later. We were two groups. Eddy had the younger kids, about fifty. They left first. The rest of us, immediately after, with Fred."

"Did you walk?" Renate interrupted.

"Walk? We ran! You would have, too. They were shooting at us. Man! There wasn't much left of our own troops, and those we saw were running out of ammunition. Reinforcements are constantly bombarded. Hardly anything gets through. I wouldn't want to have to fight under those circumstances. Would you believe, there was a joker, sergeant or some such rank, who wanted to keep us there? He kept on yelling at Fred, 'I need these men!' meaning us, and Fred yelled back, 'These are my children! They are entrusted to me!' It was hilarious, I tell you. We got away from him pretty fast.

"We caught up with the others at the railroad tracks. There was a Red Cross train, carrying mainly wounded, but a few cars were also packed with troops. That's against the rules of the Geneva Convention. The train had been stuck there, but suddenly it was moving very slowly, but moving. Everything became total madness from that moment on. I don't know where all those people suddenly came from. But I swear there were thousands, all trying to get on this train. And there wasn't any room. You've never heard such screaming. Everyone screamed. Officers were shouting orders that no one could hear anymore—and Fred. Fred yelled louder than anyone! 'The kids! Take the kids aboard! Let the kids on, for heaven's sake! We have to get the kids out of here!'

"I can still hear him and see him pushing kids on, two, three at a time. . . . I think he got them all on." Rolf stopped.

"But not you?" Renate asked quietly. "What happened?"

Rolf twisted pieces of hay around his finger. "I'm not sure what happened. There was so much shouting and screaming and the train was moving faster and no one paid any attention to the shooting, and then something exploded in the middle of the crowd. People were running in every direction when another grenade hit. I fell and then crawled under an empty oil drum. I don't know how long the shooting lasted or how long I was there. When things calmed down, I came out. It was almost dark. The train was gone, and so was everyone else—except, of course, the dead."

He did not say anything for a long time, and when he spoke again, his voice was devoid of emotion. "I passed the train the next day. Not much left of it. All bombed-out and burned. After the bombers, fighter planes must have come, strafing every moving thing. There wasn't a living soul in sight—only corpses. Plenty of them."

"Since then you've been by yourself?"

"*Hm*, and I'll keep walking and hiding until I'm home . . . if there still is a home." He looked at her, opening his eyes wide. "Say! I don't even know your name!"

"Renate. Renate Wenkenberg."

"Renate is no name for you!"

"Why not?"

"Because I don't like Renate, but I like you. Let me see . . ." He cocked his head this way and that as he studied her. "Elvira? No . . . Hanna? Hanna, maybe . . . it

27

should be something classic. . . ."

"Why?"

"*Ssshht!* Don't interrupt me. Beate? Martina? Matilda? Matilda, Matilda. Yes. That's it. You are Matilda."

"No, I'm not."

"Yes, you are, Matilda. Matilda! Matilda!"

"Renate, Renate! Renate!" she said.

Matilda, Matilda, Renate, Renate. They tried to out-shout each other. In his effort to speak louder and faster than she, MatildaMatildamatilda turned into Mtildatildatilda and Tillatillatilla, Tilla. "Tilla! Tilla! Tilla! Tilla!" he yelled, long after she had given up. Hopping up and down in the hay, he kept on repeating, "Tilla! Tilla! Tilla!"

"I like that," she said.

They were quiet then, listened to the noise of planes, as V formation after V formation passed overhead.

"On their way to Berlin," he said. "These bastards will be there before us."

9 The cold east wind blew his white hair. Dr. Martin Kohler shivered as he searched for his keys. He felt especially tired tonight. It was de-pressing not to be able to deal the right way with even the most common injuries and diseases. Medication, like every-thing else, was scarce, certain salves and antibiotics being almost impossible to get. The only pharmacy in town had run out of bandages and cotton. The armed forces, though they had priority, didn't have any either. He had been to the military hospital, the old school building turned infirmary. A pitiful place, which lacked all facilities normally associated with a hospital. Depressing to see the disillusioned, battle-weary wounded and not be able to give them anything but the most rudimentary care.

Depressing, too, the hordes of frightened, haggard refugees and their tales of horror. He did not doubt that most of what they related was true. Misery, death, destruction. Germany was getting what it deserved. The common prayer now was: "Better an end with horror than horror without end." He knew it would come all too true.

And today they had started to tear up the pavement in the center of town, right by the post office. It had taken him awhile to figure out what the soldiers were doing, or rather why. Only after watching Hitler Youth boys place sandbags along the edge of the trench had he understood that they were digging trenches. Digging trenches!

As far as he had been able to make out, they were no deeper than three feet and no wider than two. Ridiculous was the only fitting description. Yet he knew the Nazis, who gave these orders, to be serious. He knew they would also expect him and other old men, along with the boys, to defend Sonnewalde (population 4,500), Sonnewalde and the fatherland. The old, the lame, and the children would be expected to fight and save a Germany that was already lost.

His spirits lightened, as they always did, when he entered

his house. It was an oasis, now more than ever before.

From the living room came the warm, rich sounds of the venerable old Bechstein. Marianne, his wife, was playing the piano. He tried to be quiet, didn't want to interrupt her, but that was an impossibility with Rufus around. The big black Newfoundland dog came bounding up to him. Marianne stopped and came out to greet him.

They had had a quiet, simple dinner and now, still enjoying a glass of wine, said again what they had said so many times before. They might have been reading from a script, so exactly did their words match those of the night before. He wanted her to be safe, and West Germany was safer because the Western Allies would be the occupation troops. Her sister lived there; she'd be welcome. But Marianne refused to listen, refused to go anywhere without him. The argument ended predictably with: "I'm not leaving without you, Martin."

"You know that I cannot leave here."

"I know. That's why I'm staying."

Once again they had reached that point. He was about to take her hand when Rufus growled, then barked and ran to the door.

They had found a moaning boy, sitting slumped over on the baggage rack of a bicycle, and a girl holding the bike with great effort. The boy was so light and thin that Dr. Kohler, despite his age, was easily able to lift him and carry him to his office.

The girl had not wanted to come. She had stood there, wide-eyed in her muddy coat and pants, hay all over her, clutching the bike.

Marianne poured herself another glass of wine, leaned back into the soft corner of the velvet sofa. "How fortunate we have been, Martin," she said. "They could have forced us to take people in; but they didn't, and it has worked out just right for these two that the children's rooms are empty. Remember when ours were that age? I'm certainly glad that the boy is all right, but I wonder . . . Do you think that the girl is telling the truth? I cannot imagine anyone so mean or even crazy that they'd tell a young girl her mother and brother roasted to death 'like Easter lambs.' Her voice was so matter-of-fact when she told me, it was eerie."

"You must understand," Dr. Kohler said, "that they are in shock. They don't know it, but they are. We faint when physical pain becomes greater than our threshold for it. Something similar happens with emotional pain. The mind sets up a roadblock, so to speak. The reality, what actually happened, is either completely blocked or allowed only to get through in a trickle.

"They talk about what has happened to them, but they comprehend it only superficially. If they were able to realize —fully to comprehend—all at once, they'd go mad, as mad as the man who told Tilla about her mother and brother. If the realization comes gradually, painful as it is, they may be able to cope with it."

Mrs. Kohler sighed. "Can one ever cope, hope to cope with the fact that one is all alone in the world, Martin? Alone in the worst of times?"

"I don't know, Marianne. I really don't know. Let's hope that they'll get to Berlin safely. Let's hope that the aunt is still alive."

"What about the boy?"

"He didn't want to talk about who it is he has in Berlin, and I didn't want to press him."

10 Tilla and Rolf had been frightened by the enemy planes which droned overhead. Rolf, followed by Tilla, had crawled back into the hay. They had tunneled themselves into the very center of the warm, dry grass where Rolf had his knapsack and blanket.

"That looks cozy! How long have you been here?" Tilla asked.

"Since early this morning. I was just going to sleep for a while when I saw you coming. I'll wait here till it's dark, then on to Berlin. Come sit down," he offered. "There's enough room."

"Why at night?" Tilla asked. "Why can't we go together, during daylight? I can take you on my baggage rack."

"That would be the day," he scoffed. "You, a girl, pedal, and I, in uniform, sit behind you. . . . You're crazy! Besides, I've already told you why I can't be seen. If they catch me. . . ." He let the sentence trail off, then added quietly, "I don't want to fight."

"I can't imagine that you'd—"

"There are lots of things you can't imagine!"

"I've got to be going soon," Tilla said after a pause. "I came here just to be out of the wind for a bit and—"

He interrupted. "You know what I would like right now—what I would like more than anything in the world?"

"What?"

"Chocolate pudding with vanilla sauce," came the prompt answer. "You like chocolate pudding?"

She thought awhile before answering, "I like it the other way around. I mean, my favorite is vanilla pudding with chocolate sauce. Isn't that funny?" They both laughed. "But listen"—she was suddenly serious—"I have an apple. We can share it." Reaching into her canvas bag, she brought out the brown, shriveled apple, then the tin plate and the knife. "It doesn't look so good," she said apologetically. "Maybe it will taste better than it looks."

"You eat it. Go ahead, eat it," Rolf said. "I'm not hungry."

"You have to take it," Tilla insisted, holding out half the apple. "I can't eat if you don't."

"Yes, you can. You want to bet that you can? You will eat your apple, and I shall read to you."

"Read? Read what?"

"I shall read to you from *The Call of the Wild*, a very fine story to eat an apple to." After much rummaging around in his knapsack, he found what he had been looking for and triumphantly held up a ragged, dog-eared book, which was wrapped in plain paper. "It's really good! I swear you'll like it. Now eat your apple." And he began:

Buck did not read the newspapers, or he would

have known that trouble was brewing, not alone for himself, but for every tidewater dog, strong of muscle and with warm, long hair, from Puget Sound to San Diego.

Rolf looked up to see that Tilla had put her hand over her ears.

"I can't stand it! I'm so hungry I can't stand it. Unless you eat the other half, I won't eat mine. I can't eat by myself," she said stubbornly, "but you don't care if I starve, do you?"

"But I do," he said earnestly. "I really do. It's just . . . I'm afraid."

"Afraid of half of one lousy apple?"

"Don't be silly! I'm afraid that if I eat it, I'll really get hungry." He flipped the pages of the book. "It's been so long. I don't even remember when I last had something to eat. It's been so long that I'm not hungry anymore."

"But you must eat!" Tilla said with alarm. "You have to eat *something!*"

Sitting side by side on the blanket in the hay, they ate the apple, and after that their stomachs woke up, growled, and demanded food. It was then that they started on the potatoes, peeled first one, chewed it, liked it, then another, and kept on peeling and chewing.

They ate greedily, Rolf so fast that he had eaten ten by the time Tilla munched on her sixth. While trying to convince her that they should travel together, at night, he finished a full dozen raw potatoes.

Tilla agreed, except that she wanted to travel by day. She argued her point vehemently, insisted that nothing would happen to him—they'd both be on the lookout—and she even offered to let him ride the bike and she would sit on the baggage rack.

One as stubborn as the other, they kept arguing until the shed threw a long shadow. Noon had turned into afternoon. There was not enough left of the day to make good progress, Tilla knew, and she gave in to Rolf when he said, "Listen, we'll try both, my way tonight, yours tomorrow. All right? We'll see how far we get and how it goes. Now," he added happily, "I can read to you until it's dark."

It was nice to have found a friend. She had liked him from the start. Curled up and surrounded by the fragrance of hay, she relaxed and was soon engrossed in the fate of the dog Buck. The beautiful black dog Buck, who had been kidnapped, tortured, and beaten and was facing yet another nightmare.

Rolf read:

No lazy, sun-kissed life was this, with nothing to do but loaf and be bored. Here was neither peace, nor rest, nor a moment's safety.

Tilla knew exactly what it meant, felt with all her heart for Buck, listening to Rolf read.

"All was confusion and—" Rolf suddenly groaned, doubled over, holding his stomach. Moans and groans answered Tilla's questions. He was obviously in pain, in

35

such pain that he rolled around in the hay, making the most heartbreaking noises.

Tilla pleaded, "Please hang on! Hang on, and I'll try to get you to a doctor," not knowing what else to do. A doctor seemed the only remedy. "Hang on, I'll hurry," she kept on repeating, while she quickly rolled up the blanket, strapped it to his knapsack, tucked the book into a side pocket, and then gathered her own things. She took the bike out, hung the knapsack and her now much lighter potato bag on the handlebar, and somehow managed to get him outside. Supporting him, she reached the road, where he got onto the baggage rack of her bike, like an obedient child.

SONNEWALDE—1 mile / BERLIN—85 miles. Luckily it was downhill all the way to the village. No one took any notice of the boy and girl on the bike. A group of small children directed her to Dr. Kohler's house.

11 The soft candlelight made the wine in the crystal glasses sparkle. Dr. Kohler and his wife quietly talked about the sleeping girl and boy upstairs. The conversation turned to their own children, grown-up now and far away. They recalled the funny moments they had had, the adventures and good times.

"Shall I open another bottle?" the doctor asked.

Marianne smiled. "Yes. One of the Niersteiner Domtal,

Martin. This is a very special night. Who knows how many more will be granted us?"

"*Sssht!*" The doctor put a finger to his lips. "Let's not worry about tomorrow. It'll come all too soon."

"You know," Marianne said as he was uncorking the bottle, "I've been thinking . . . could we keep them here?"

"They'll want to go home," he replied. "I mean," the doctor corrected himself quickly, "they will want to find their relatives. They should. We can't take the responsibility of keeping them here when we ourselves don't know what's in store. It may be months or only a matter of weeks until the Russians are here. What will happen then? They belong with their own. Their families would never forgive us, and rightly so." He paused. "Still, I suppose a few days of rest and some decent meals can't hurt. But then they should leave and find their people."

"What if there's no one left to find? You know what's happening in Berlin! Air raids day and night. One can't imagine that there's anything or anyone left in that town."

"It's bad, but not that bad. Maybe I can find someone who is going to Berlin and can give them a lift. We can tell them to come back to us if they don't find their own families. Maybe it will help them to know that they can come back. They are certainly nice and well mannered."

"They certainly are," Marianne said, and there was an edge to her voice. "But what difference does it make whether they're well brought up or not? They are alone in these times when no one gives a damn!"

"We'll make them stay a few days, so you can fatten them up."

"I'm glad that I married a doctor"—Marianne laughed—"a country doctor whose patients pay with produce instead of cash. That comes in handy at a time like this. To your health, Martin!"

"To yours, Marianne!"

They touched glasses. The clear sound of the crystal was suddenly interrupted by a timid cough. Rufus woke up and began to bark.

"I'm sorry," said Rolf, after Rufus had calmed down. "May I please have a glass of water? I am awfully thirsty."

"But of course, of course!" said the couple.

"Come on down," said Marianne. "Are you feeling better? Maybe you're ready for a bit of hot stew now?"

"I'm fine. Stew would be great if you can spare some."

Rolf slowly came downstairs, so as not to trip over the flannel shirt, which covered him down to his naked feet. The sleeves hung so long and limp that he gave the impression of not having any arms.

They wrapped him in one of the two mohair blankets on the sofa, and after Marianne had heated the vegetable stew, they watched him like anxious parents, making sure that he ate slowly.

"You don't have to eat that!" Marianne pointed to a piece of gristle. "Leave that to Rufus. Rufus! Rufus?"

"He's right here," Tilla answered from the upstairs landing. She was sitting there with her arms wrapped around Rufus's strong, furry neck and her small, pale face nuzzled up against his big black one.

"Come down and join us, you two!" said the doctor.

"Looks as if we're going to have an impromptu midnight party."

"I couldn't sleep," Tilla said, as she descended as carefully as Rolf had. She, too, wore one of the doctor's long-sleeved flannel shirts and in it looked like Rolf's twin. "I was going to look for Rolf's book." She kissed Rufus on the nose. "Doesn't he look like Buck, Rolf?"

"He does," agreed Rolf, and added, "I've been reading to Tilla about this dog named Buck. *The Call of the Wild* is the title of the story."

"Jack London!" the doctor and his wife said together, and looked pleased.

"Splendid story," said the doctor.

Marianne walked along the bookshelves that covered one whole wall until she found a slender volume, exquisitely bound in sea blue leather. She handed it to Tilla, who hardly dared touch it.

"How does the story end?" Tilla wanted to know.

"You mean you didn't finish it? Maybe the doctor will read it to us? I would like to hear it again, too. He's very good at that," Marianne added.

"If the lady of the house can come up with another plate of stew for Tilla while I look for my glasses, I'll be glad to."

"All we need now is a fire in the fireplace," Marianne remarked after she had brought the stew. "But we can't. Enemy planes might see the sparks and mistake us for an industrial plant."

"Shall I start at the beginning?" the doctor asked. He was answered by an unanimous yes. He read the story of Buck,

39

beautiful strong black son of a St. Bernard and Scotch shepherd. Read how the dog was kidnapped, of his struggle to stay alive in a merciless environment in bitter-cold Alaska, and of the treatment, fair as well as cruel, he received.

Rolf and Tilla, on the sofa, were bundled up so tightly in the mohair blankets that they resembled cocoons. Marianne, occasionally stealing a glance, noticed how enthralled they were by the story—even Rolf, who obviously knew it. Each ordeal the story dog went through was reflected on their faces. They seemed to have forgotten about themselves and were suffering with Buck. But both also fought a fight with sleep and heavy eyelids. By the time Buck came into kind hands and happy times Tilla was fast asleep. The doctor picked her up and carried her to bed.

Rolf was still fighting a valiant battle to stay awake but losing fast. "Thank you, thank you very much," he whispered, and wondered how to tell these nice people that he had to leave, but now that Tilla was asleep, he would have to wait. . . .

"Up to bed with you, too—and sleep well," they said.

"Good night and thank you," said Rolf, unable to resist the lure of the clean, comfortable bed and a good night's rest.

12 The next morning Tilla and Rolf found a breakfast waiting that made them wonder whether they were still in a dream. Marianne had to urge and nudge them to sit down, so transfixed were they by the sight of a table holding an abundance of food they had not seen in years.

There were two bowls, steaming with hot oats, a basket with fresh, warm rolls Marianne had baked. A huge slab of sweet yellow butter sat on a plate next to a jar of home-made strawberry jam and a crock of golden honey. Crocheted cozies in the form of chickens kept two soft-boiled eggs warm. There was a pitcher of milk and a large, very full sugar bowl.

Tilla and Rolf were hesitant at first, taking tiny bites and only an infinitesimal amount of the delicious jam, no more than a drop or two of honey, and all but counting the sugar grains, one by one, into the oats. The habit of many years of rationing.

"You're not eating!" Marianne said, exasperated. "All of this is for you," she assured them. "Please! Will you please help yourselves!"

Two hands reached for the rolls and pulled back quickly. "After you," said Rolf.

"No, no," Tilla protested. "You take that one." And then they settled down to the serious business of eating.

If Marianne had found it difficult to assure Tilla and Rolf that all this wonderful food had been put on the table for them, she found it impossible to convince them that it would be better for them to stay a few days.

Tilla confounded the doctor's wife by putting everything she owned on the kitchen table. Before Marianne understood, Tilla lined up twenty-eight potatoes and three onions, slipped a ten-mark bill and two ones under the onions, and laid fifty pfennig in change next to it. Rolf added four crumbled one-mark bills and thirty pfennig in change.

Marianne, for the first time in her life, was at a loss for words, didn't know whether she should laugh or cry. *It's come to that,* she thought. *No one can accept a bit of human kindness without thinking that he has to pay for it.* She looked at them as they stood before her with such serious faces. She reached out and hugged them to her as she had hugged her own, a long time ago, and cried. She held them until she felt herself in control again. "You'll just have to put up with me," she finally said. "I didn't know myself how much I've missed having children around." Marianne, still sniffling, released them. "Take your—take this all off the table, please!"

"We know we can't pay you for what you've done," Rolf said, shuffling his feet uneasily. "It's embarrassing . . . but we also can't just accept all this, that you've let us stay here and all the food, with everything being rationed. We don't know what to do. That's all we have."

Marianne went so far as to show them the pantry (one of three), where they gaped at the rows of sparkling jars filled with fruit and vegetables, at the sausages hanging from the ceiling, at the huge hunk of bacon and the earth-

42

enware crocks of different sizes, their contents hidden and left to everyone's imagination. "You see," she told them as she closed the door behind her, "thanks to the doctor, we can afford to feed you—and us—for some time to come."

Tilla and Rolf, after much serious deliberation, then agreed to stay until they could get a ride. They wouldn't lose any time this way—and it would be safer. They would not, could not admit even to themselves that they were scared. Afraid to be once again alone out there, alone on the open road. To be cold again and hungry or sick and have no one to turn to.

They lay, with Rufus, on the carpet in the library, playing cards, laughing sometimes. They exchanged few words —and these only about the game. They would have liked to talk, but there were no words to express the terrifying images of the experiences which filled their heads. Unable to concentrate on the game, they soon gave up, played for a while with the dog, and then wandered aimlessly around the room. Tilla looked at the objects, a little silver box, small sculptures of animals, careful not to touch anything. Rolf studied the books, read titles out to her, and commented on the authors as well as on their work. *He's my age,* she thought, *how can he know all those books?* When he nonchalantly remarked that it was quite a decent library, especially for a country doctor, Tilla was truly shocked and fervently hoped Marianne hadn't heard. His boldness passed all bounds when, without asking, he dared open the baby grand, playfully hitting a key here, another there. "Stop it!" Tilla said with consternation. "You can't do that!"

"Why not?" he said, and grinned, then forced the Bechstein to emit some extraordinarily hideous sounds. "I'm a pianist!" he declared, mimed lifting the tails of a formal coat, and sat down on the piano stool. She noticed that his unusually long, bony fingers reached octaves without a problem. He played and seemed to have forgotten all about her. He really knew how to play.

Tilla lay down, resting her head on Rufus. She had never heard anyone play like this, except maybe on the radio. Marianne came in on tiptoe, sat down, taking care not to make any noise, closed her eyes, and listened. Rolf played until the doctor came home for lunch.

13 Dr. Kohler was too agitated to pay any attention to Rolf's playing. He told them that the Hitler Youth in the area was forcing even fourteen-year-olds not only to build trenches but to fight. Should they, could they hide Rolf? Or would it be better if both young people, or maybe just Rolf, left on the truck Hartfeld, the owner of the lumberyard, was sending to Berlin with a load of cement. The truck was someplace else at the moment. Hartfeld wasn't sure when it would be free, only that it would be today. And he hadn't even been sure that the driver would take them. Hartfeld had promised to talk to the driver, but he couldn't tell him what to do. He was a sergeant, and the cement was a military shipment. All he could say was that if the driver agreed, he'd be by to pick them up. If they wanted to go, they'd better be ready.

"Tonight! We'll be in Berlin tonight!" Rolf jumped with joy. Rufus barked.

Marianne cried out, "Not today! It's too soon! What if the driver isn't trustworthy and—"

"What if? What if?" the doctor said over his wife's objections. "I trust Hartfeld's judgment and. . . ." He raised his voice to be heard because Marianne was still talking. Kept on talking. Then she started crying, as did Tilla, and Rufus howled.

"We are leaving, Tilla," Rolf said calmly. "We'll be in Berlin tonight."

It was getting dark and beginning to snow lightly as the truck bounced over the rough country roads toward Berlin. In the back, squeezed in between the cement sacks, were Tilla and Rolf and the bike. They huddled close together under the big old army coat Marianne had given Rolf. They would have liked to talk but could not make themselves heard over the din of engine and wind. Rolf, his arm protectively around Tilla, pulled the coat tighter together. As she turned her head, their noses touched.

The warmth made their bodies feel like one, and a strange feeling came over them. The world shrank until only they existed in the descending darkness. They looked into each other's eyes. Who could outstare whom? And then Rolf kissed her.

45

To judge by the effect, she might have been struck by lightning and would have jumped clear into the air if she could have. But his arms kept her seated in the small space they occupied between the mountains of immovable sacks. She struggled mightily until he released his grip and looked at her with that peculiar expression of his, a mixture between grin and smile. He said something which she couldn't understand. He repeated it louder, and she still couldn't make it out. Then he took a deep breath, opened his mouth, and "NEVER!" rang out over the dark, quiet village street as truck and motor had abruptly stopped. "NEVER!" echoed back from the small houses. "Never," he now whispered into her ear, "will I do that again—unless you like it!" and both doubled over with laughter.

The driver slammed the door of the cab. They heard his steps, but it was too dark to see him. "Are you crazy?" he snarled as dogs began to bark. "Stupid! To wake up the whole neighborhood! . . . Listen, I'm gonna have a beer. If you wanna come in, it's all right by me. Might warm you up a bit," he added in a friendlier voice.

Because of the blackout, there were no outside lights, but they saw his silhouette, for a moment, as he entered what seemed to be a restaurant.

They climbed off the truck and groped their way to the door, opened it, and were met by a solid wall of smoke and noise.

It was one of those low-ceilinged small-town restaurant-bars. Undistinguished in every way—therefore timeless. A place where local laborers gather to relax for an evening or, more often, where they came to drown their never-ending worries. It was packed—soldiers mostly, old men, too, and a few women.

There was raucous laughter at the bar, where they stood three deep. "Is this kiddy night, Al?" someone shouted as everyone turned to the door.

Among the crowd at the bar, towering over anyone there, was a big bear of a soldier, who now beckoned "Come here!" to Rolf, who stepped forward. Tilla followed. "One light one, Al!" he told the bartender. "I wanna buy my buddy here a beer," his voice boomed as he slapped Rolf on the back.

"Can't do that," the grizzled little bartender said. "Can't serve liquor to minors."

"Minors? Hell!" The bear was obviously drunk. "He's not a minor; he's my comrade! And I wanna buy him a beer 'cause he and I are gonna defend the fatherland! Aren't we, buddy?" Rolf nodded, and the bear put his big arm around Rolf's narrow shoulders. "Where's that beer for my buddy, Al?" the bear demanded as his fist hit the counter.

"Take it easy, Bert!" some of the men mumbled, and Al, wiping the counter wtih a dirty rag, replied, "I told you, Bert, I can't do it. He's not old enough!"

"Not *old* enough!" The bear's voice had now reached its full volume, and he swayed slightly. "Old enough. Old enough to fight, old enough to drink, that's what I say— ain't that right?" He blinked, looked at the men around him, but had trouble focusing. He leaned heavily on the counter. "Goddammit, Al! Where's that beer? An' a

47

schnapps for me. Enjoy while you can, right, comrade?" He gave Rolf another slap, knocking him against some bystanders. "Here's a man in uniform," the bear growled, pointing his finger at Rolf's chest, "and Al refuses the man a beer—goddammit, Al!" he shouted. "Where is it?"

Al, without looking up, pushed a beer and a small glass of schnapps toward the bear, whose big hand reached for the small glass and handed it to Rolf. He took the beer. "Cheers, comrade." His glass clinked against Rolf's. "You and I are going to beat the pants off the Russians—right?" Whip their asses all the way back to Moscow!" With that he lifted his glass, never taking his eyes off Rolf, and downed the beer in one long, continuous gulp.

Rolf politely lifted the small glass, seemed to study the clear liquid for a moment before he tossed the contents into his open mouth. He shut his mouth, swallowed hard; then his eyes widened and got moist. He shuddered once, as if shaken from within.

"Bravo!" said the bear, and loudly clapped his hands. "Told you, Al, he's a man!"

"A very cute one at that!" said a coarse, husky female voice. It belonged to a woman with bleached hair and lips of such ruby red that they looked as if they were bleeding. She had elbowed her way into the crowd at the bar, all but pushed Tilla aside, so she could stand next to Rolf. "Old enough to fight, old enough to . . ." She winked at Rolf and laughed. "How about it, 'soldier'?" Rolf beamed.

Tilla, though she didn't know why, hated that woman, hated her flabby flesh, hated that powdered face with the blue veins in the cheeks, hated the whole, monstrous apparition. But Rolf, as if flattered, smiled knowingly. Grinned as if he knew exactly what the woman was talking about . . . and turned that grin on Tilla. The woman's eyes followed.

"That your girl friend?" she asked.

"That's my sister," he answered, and Tilla couldn't understand why this upset her. "Isn't she cute?" he added, and sensed that Tilla wanted to get out, get away from there, so he playfully took her hand, before she could turn, and drew her close and repeated to her, "You *are* cute!" and kissed her on the cheek—in front of all those people.

The bear, elbow propped on the counter, head in his hand, appeared to have fallen asleep.

"Get those kids outa here!" Al growled from behind the bar. "Whose kids are they anyway?"

The answer came from a far corner of the room. "They're on my truck. I'm taking them to Berlin." Slowly, reluctantly, the driver made his way toward the bar.

"Get 'em the hell outa here," said Al. "This is no place for kids! You know that!"

"They're not exactly kids!" the driver said apologetically. "Thought they might warm up for a bit."

For the first time, Rolf and Tilla got a good look at him —as good a look as possible under the circumstances. He was a small, stocky man in his forties, and it wasn't just the sergeant's uniform—the whole man looked wrinkled. Wrinkled, unkempt, and slightly soiled. His graying hair, though short-cropped, was untidy, too. His face was broad, almost square, but it had a weasel-like quality, maybe because of the small, darting eyes or maybe because there was a certain nervousness about him, even when he moved slowly.

"Don't you have anything hot for 'em?" he now asked Al.

"Like what?"

"I don't know . . . hot chocolate or something?"

"Hot chocolate!" Al bellowed as if this were the best joke he'd heard in years. "Hot chocolate! Hot chocolate he wants for the little darlings!" He guffawed as others started to join in the laughter. "Anyone seen any chocolate lately?" He addressed the crowd and received the scornful laughter he had expected in reply.

"Sure!" The bleached blonde giggled. "I saw some in 1938—no, wait, it must have been . . ." But no one listened. She was drowned out by jokes and comments that came from all corners of the room.

"You gotta have something hot for 'em!" the driver shouted angrily over the din. "Hot broth, tea—anything!"

"I've got something hot for you, honey!"

It was the bleached blonde, talking to Rolf, but Tilla heard it, and so did the driver, who snapped. "Old sow! You oughta be ashamed of yourself!"

The blonde didn't have a chance to reply, for a very fat woman appeared between them and fixed Tilla and Rolf with eyes like shiny, small black beads. "I'll get you something," she said, and disappeared.

"Better make it quick," the driver shouted after her. "I gotta get going." Then he turned to Rolf and asked, "Got any money?"

"Sure," said Rolf.

"How much?"

"Enough!"

The fat woman returned with two cups that slopped over as she set them on the counter, and the liquid ran against the bear's elbow. But he was soundly asleep by now and certainly beyond the triviality of a wet elbow. "Mark-fifty. Who's paying?" the woman wanted to know.

Rolf reached into his pocket and produced two of his crumpled bills, which the fat woman swept up. By the time Tilla had found her money purse the change was already on the counter.

"Put it away, sis," said Rolf. "We'll get even later." And he had the audacity to wink at her.

They drank the lukewarm contents of the cups. It was impossible to determine what it was other than that it was dark, clear, and salty. The driver sniffed and disgustedly wrinkled his nose. "That's what she calls broth, I suppose. Well, what the hell? Better than a kick in the teeth. Come on. Let's go."

14 White searchlights fingered the sky over the dark village. They inhaled the cool, fresh air with an appreciative long drawn-out *aah*. A short-lived joy, for the driver decided that Tilla and Rolf should ride with him in the cab of the truck.

"Gotta plan ahead," he explained. "Chances are there'll

be an air raid. You'd be sitting ducks in the back—take forever to climb off." He held the door to let them in first; then he got behind the big, cumbersome steering wheel as they squeezed together in the other seat. "Try the handle," he told Rolf, "so that you know how to open it." Rolf did. "Awright, you can close it now. That's the side you get off, unnerstand? When I stop, you run! Look for shelter . . . main thing's get off the road! Got that?"

The cab stank. The driver's own odor dominated over that of cheap, stale tobacco, car grease, sweaty leather, and a whole variety of undefinable unpleasant smells. The instrument panel lights were blissfully dim, hinting at, rather than showing, the general chaos of rags, maps, packages and whatnot which filled the cab of the truck from top to bottom. They bounced and bumped along, following the blue shine of the hooded headlights.

All three of them saw it at the same moment. The truck came to such a sudden stop that they were thrown forward and all manner of things flew about.

The barricade, a primitive wooden thing, stood in the middle of the road, visible only when the blue flashlights pointed at it. "Shit!" said the driver. "Chaindogs!" He opened the door and stepped down to meet them.

It was immediately apparent what the driver meant by "chaindogs" because the soldiers who now inspected his papers by flashlight wore large chains around their necks, chains with a flat medallion in the center. They looked medieval and mean when a light flashed by one or the other. Their nailed boots clattering over the cobblestones, two of the soldiers went to the back and climbed on the truck. Another, with a voice so cold it sent shivers down their spines, asked the driver, "Who've you got in there?"

"Two kids," the driver answered.

The soldier motioned to them and said, "Out!"

Their eyes had adjusted enough to see clearly the pistol in his waving hand. As soon as they stood in front of him, the pistol pointed at Rolf's chest.

Rolf didn't wait for the voice to speak but reported, military fashion, "Severin, Rolf Andreas, Hitler Youth Troop Eighteen—Berlin Center," and clicked his heels.

"Papers!" the voice demanded.

"Lost, doing relief work in Dresden," Rolf replied crisply, and went on to explain in short, precise sentences that he had been given orders to report to his unit at Berlin Center.

Though Tilla was so scared that she didn't dare breathe, Rolf seemed so completely calm and so believable that she wondered whether he hadn't made up what he had told her.

"And *you?*" the spine-chilling voice asked as the pistol waved in her direction.

"That's my sister," Rolf replied for her, making her feel childish and dumb.

The flashlight quickly swept her face. Then there came a grunt, and the chaindog walked away. He walked to the back of the truck, where they heard him talk to the others.

Driver, Tilla and Rolf stood stock-still, straining their ears, but couldn't make out what was being said. Then, boots clacking, the chaindogs returned.

"All right! Move!" said the chill voice, and the pistol was still waving through the air.

They hurried, glad even to get back into the stinking truck cab, and they sighed with relief when the old engine came back to life and the barricade was removed. With the eerie blue-green light of the instruments casting a glow, they rumbled off into the night.

The driver, obviously intent on avoiding another road-block, turned here and there, bounced the old truck through narrow back alleys of small towns and over roads that were merely dirt paths, then suddenly stopped at what looked like a lumberyard. "You stay here," he said as he got out and disappeared into the night.

"What's happening now?" Tilla whispered. But Rolf put a finger over her lips as they heard a whistle. It sounded like someone whistling for his dog. One long sound, fol-lowed by two short ones. Then a door creaked, and they could hear two men talking. One was the driver, who re-turned shortly thereafter, saying, "Whatta you say, kids? Wanna call it a night? You can catch a couple hours of shut-eye here with my friend."

After retrieving bicycle, bag, knapsack, and coat, they followed the driver through a maze of stacked lumber to the back entrance of a building. It turned out to be a small hotel or pension. It was evident, even by the dim emergency light, that it was a simple but well-run place. Orderly piles of bed and table linens lay on a bench; trash cans stood in a neat file, ready to be taken out. Everything was very clean and tidy.

A gaunt middle-aged woman, pink bathrobe over long

flowered nightgown, came slowly down the stairs, yawning widely. Her face, once she'd closed her mouth, was so devoid of expression it might have been a mask. Only her eyes moved when she addressed the driver in a querulous voice: "I told you, Max, I have only one room left! You didn't say that they were boy and girl!"

"One's enough for 'em, Emma! They're brother and sister. We've only got a couple hours anyway."

After a long look at Rolf and Tilla the woman shrugged her shoulders, nodded, and yawned again. "There's only this one bed, but they're skinny . . . guess it'll do." She paused. "Are you paying for them, Max?"

"They have money," said the driver.

"How much is it?" asked Rolf.

"Ten mark," came the prompt answer. "Can't let it go for less. What with the sheets and the towels and all, I'm hardly making any money as it is." Tilla had found her money more quickly this time. *That's what I was supposed to use it for,* she thought, *but then there hadn't been any Rolf.* She watched the woman stuff the ten-mark bill into the pocket of the pink bathrobe. *What if I say that he isn't my brother?* flashed through her mind. But she didn't say it, instead said, "Thank you," to the woman's offer to leave the bike in the hallway, and was the first to follow the woman upstairs when she said, "Come on then, I'll show you the room."

There was a long corridor, with many doors, but they stopped in front of the first, which had a black number 6 painted on it.

"Night then," the driver called from below, and they

55

heard him open and close the back door, heard his heavy steps on the gravel outside.

"There you are," said the woman, and switched on a small blue ceiling light. "I'll wake you when Max is ready."

Suddenly they were alone—alone in a hotel room where everything looked bluish. Bed and nightstand, dresser and chair, washbasin, and even Rolf looked blue in the light of the emergency bulb. A lonely wooden coat hanger dangled from a peg on the wall. "Hotel Savoy" was imprinted on it.

"Look!" Rolf pointed to the painting over the bed. "Look at our guardian angels! See how happy they are?"

She looked at the smiling, fat angels, cavorting amid clouds, and nodded.

He asked, "Aren't you going to take off your coat?" as he took off his uniform jacket and shoes.

She didn't move, stood wide-eyed and confused. She was tired, wanted to lie down, wanted to be near Rolf, desperately desired that nearness, the warmth she had felt when they were huddled together on the truck. But in the back of her mind, a small voice said, *It's wrong! You're not supposed to do that! You're not supposed to feel that way.* So she stood quite still, Emil Troester's World War I canvas bag over her shoulder, clutching the bag with the remaining twenty-eight potatoes, and three onions and the parcel from the doctor's wife. How to undress and get into that bed *with* Rolf there? She didn't know what to do.

He tiptoed toward her, skinny legs in rough knee stockings, asking softly, "Tilla? Are you afraid, Tilla?" She nodded violently, and big tears started to roll down her cheeks.

"You are afraid of me, Tilla?" he asked, and gently embraced her, leaned his head against hers, and whispered, "I won't hurt you! You know I won't! Stop crying! Please. Everything is going to be all right. We've found each other, and now we'll always stay together—yes?" She nodded just a little bit, and he went on, "The war will be over, and I'll become a pianist, and you'll be a famous movie star!"

"I don't want to be a movie star!" she said defiantly, so like a stubborn child that he almost laughed.

He held her by the shoulders and looked into her eyes. "What do you want to be?"

"I want to be an artist. I've always wanted to be an artist."

"Oh, Tilla! That's beautiful! It's going to be beautiful. We'll have a big apartment with French louver doors and parquet floors and a grand piano and lots of books and Oriental carpets like Dr. Kohler's. While I practice, you'll be next door in your studio, painting. And your studio will have a huge skylight."

"And I want a large fish tank," Tilla added, "with all kinds of different fish, even an angelfish!"

"Of course, my angel!" he said, taking the bag from her hand and the other one off her shoulder. He put them on the floor and helped her out of her coat. She got out of her sweater and sat down on the bed to take off her shoes. Then, like a flash, she was under the blanket, pulled it up to her chin, smiled at him with her big gray eyes.

After he had switched off the light, she heard the rustle of clothing, and then he was under the cover with her. A naked arm reached around her. His breath was warm and moist on her ear when he said, "Do you always sleep with your clothes on?"

His slender, bony body pressed against hers; hands fumbled at the waistband of the long pants she still wore. Her heart beat loud and fast as he pulled them down, despite her resistance, and the bed suddenly made such frightful creaking noises that they both lay still for a moment.

When he stroked her chest, her face grew hot for shame that it was as flat as his. She didn't move, allowed his fingers to explore her nipples, move down her belly, but when they went farther down, she pressed her thighs together as hard as she could. Still, unaccountably, one of the fingers slipped through, reached down and into the forbidden zone. His kiss stopped her exasperated sigh.

Her hand was moved, made to hold something, held firmly when it wanted to recoil. What she felt was warm, throbbing, and both soft and hard. It grew bigger, harder in her hand until . . . her hand was pushed away. He shuddered, sighed, handled, and held it with both his hands. There was a strange smell. Then he turned and suddenly covered her face with kisses, mumbling, "Angel, Tillangel, I'm sorry," and, "Thank you," and all kinds of incomprehensible things.

She was excited and embarrassed, sensed, but didn't even know how to ask, what had happened.

He got up, and she listened as he felt his way around in the dark, heard him wash, and then he was next to her once more, smelling strongly of cheap soap, a smell that contrasted sharply with that other one.

58

"Rolf? What happened . . . what did you . . . ?"

She knew he was smiling as he put his arms around her, tucked the blanket under her, and answered, just as she had anticipated, in the voice and manner of a man, "*Psst!* You innocent angel, when you become a woman, you'll know. Tell me, have you had your period?"

There was no answer because she was much too shocked —and ashamed. No one, not even her mother, had asked that, talked about it. He interpreted her silence rightly. "You haven't had it yet?" She shook her head. "That's all right. Don't worry about it. It'll all happen in time, angel."

It was comforting to lie snuggled close to him, too comforting. *It's wrong. I shouldn't do this,* she thought, but then, what had she done? Why should there be anything wrong, snuggling with a boy you liked?

"Rolf?"

"Yes, angel?"

"Is your mother still alive?"

"I don't know."

"You don't know?"

"I haven't heard from her in over five months!"

After a long pause she asked, "In Berlin, do you live far from me? I mean far from Hermsdorf?"

"Don't know. I don't know where I'll live. We were bombed out. Lost everything. She wasn't sure whether she'd find another apartment, didn't know where she'd live. Said she'd write once she knew—but she never did."

"But where will you go when we get to Berlin?"

"To the newspaper where she works. If she isn't there,

59

someone will know where she is. Listen! Do you hear what I hear?"

The unmistakable drone of airplane motors was there again, now and then interrupted by the staccato of antiair-craft-gun fire. It propelled them out of bed and made them get dressed in record time. But no siren gave alarm, and they decided to wait until it came.

Tilla listened at the door for noises of people going to a shelter. Rolf, at the window, peeked past the black paper blind, then called her over.

"Do you see what I see?"

At first she saw only a searchlight sweep over the sky, but at a particular point it illuminated the lumberyard and truck for a second. "Someone is stealing the cement bags off the truck!" Tilla said, alarmed. "We have to get the driver!"

"I don't think so," Rolf whispered. "Watch!"

Once more, and again and again, each time the search-light passed a certain spot, lumberyard and truck were momentarily visible, as were the two men who unloaded, then carted away first one bag, then another and another.

"Do you recognize the short one? It's Max, our driver. He's got a little private deal going here."

"In the middle of the night?"

"Is there a better time? He's 'diverting' or, to be precise, 'stealing' military matériel for private use. If he's caught, they'll shoot him—or hang him."

"Oh, my God!"

"That's why he was so concerned that we should get some

'shut-eye.' Idiotic expression! He didn't want to tell us before that he would stop because he didn't want us to ask questions."

The searchlight was suddenly switched off. Everything was dark, stayed dark, but the noise of the cart on gravel continued.

Suddenly hungry, they opened Marianne's package and ate first the rolls, then the cheese, and finally all of it.

15

Strips of pale gray light showed on the sides of the blackout curtain. Tilla and Rolf woke up because someone was knocking at the door, and a woman's voice called, "Get up and come on down for some coffee. Max is ready."

They found the woman and the driver in the immaculate kitchen. The woman, dressed in a heavy sweater, long skirt, and man's shoes, was pouring hot coffee into two mugs. Her face was as imperturbable as the night before. She pointed to two slices of bread with marmalade. "That's for you."

The driver, unshaved, was seated at the table, his sergeant's uniform even more crumpled than the day before. Between slurps of coffee he asked, "Well, Emma, are you running or staying?"

"Can't go and leave everything here!" she replied. "No,

Max. I'm staying, come what may." She sighed. "Where would I go anyway? And you, Max? What about you?"

"I?" he said, chewing and shrugging his shoulders. "What can I do? Gotta do my duty for Fuehrer and fatherland," he said without enthusiasm and somewhat mockingly. Then he blinked mischievously. "But you wanna bet that I'll make sure my place of duty is gonna be close to home? Very close to home."

The woman sighed. "Yes—if one still has a home, that's the place to be. I went over to the Liebers yesterday and saw what's going on . . . all those refugees! I couldn't believe my eyes! Well, I'm sure you've seen what's going on on the *Autobahn*."

"Why do you think it took me so long? Can't make time on those lousy backroads. Well, Emma"—he stretched—"I gotta get going. With luck we'll make it to the capital of our great German Reich in one piece, ha? Weather's with us. Nice heavy cloud cover. Should delay the bombers a bit. You two!" he addressed Tilla and Rolf. "Ready?" They nodded. "Well, come on then, gotta move!" He made a sound that was meant to be laughter, got up, and yawned.

"Thank you very much for the coffee and bread," said Tilla, shaking the woman's hand. "What do we owe you?"

"Ah! Forget it," the woman answered. "It was little enough. May God be with you!"

Rolf helped Tilla, then handed up the bike before he himself climbed into the truck. There was far more room, now that about a third of the cement bags were gone. They preferred being out there in the cold, by themselves, to the

62

warm stench of the cab. Arms around each other, they sat, once more, huddled under the old army greatcoat.

It was a blustery February morning. Big gray low-hanging clouds raced ominously over the sky. It was comforting to be close to someone. Tilla suddenly found herself wishing that this journey would last forever. But they were already in the outskirts of Berlin. The buildings were bigger. They were now on an asphalt highway and driving through a densely populated area. The trip would soon be over.

The truck stopped in the center of a very crowded square. Hundreds of people all seemed to be running in one direction—toward one building. The driver came around and opened the back gate.

"This is it, kids! This is Rangsdorf. That's as far as I go. Can't miss the station. Everyone else is going there, too. Berlin's fine electric trains'll take you anywhere you wanna go from here."

They got off and shook hands. "Thank you, sir," said Rolf. "I know my way from here."

"It was very kind of you to take us along," Tilla said. "We don't have much money left, but maybe you would like some potatoes?" She felt a kick at the back of her knee as she extended the bag toward the driver.

"Well," said the driver, clearing his throat and peering into the bag, "I'm certainly not gonna turn down an opportunity like this! My old lady's always complaining that she's got nothing to put on the table." He reached in, took two, three potatoes, and stuffed them into one of his pockets, while with the other, grubby hand he dug for more.

"That's enough, and thanks a lot," he remarked after the sixth. "Take care, kids!" With that he climbed into his cab, started the motor, and, waving, drove away.

"To give away your potatoes!" Rolf shook his head. "Why'd you do that?"

"Is that why you kicked me?"

"Of course! Nobody *gives away* potatoes!"

"But it was nice of him! Think of where we might be . . . and not much money left."

"I know I owe you ten!"

"That's not why I said it. The ten wasn't mine anyway. Not really."

"I won't have a girl pay for my hotel room!"

"I slept there, too," said Tilla, and blushed.

He noticed it and laughed. "All the more reason, angel!" he said, making her blush even more.

She stepped behind Rolf and said, "Don't turn," while she calculated: *Twenty-eight minus six is twenty-two, divided by two is eleven*, as she proceeded to stuff potatoes into his knapsack.

"What are you doing?"

"Stand still!" she demanded, but he whirled around.

"You are crazy!"

"No, I'm not. I want to share them with you."

"You are a crazy little girl!"

It hurt to be called a little girl when that was the last thing she wanted to be. He kissed her on the tip of her nose and added, "But I love you."

"I love you, too!" And then Rolf not only was taken

aback but almost lost his balance when she flung her arms around him, embraced him with all her might, and didn't want to let him go.

He had to extricate himself. "Come on, Tilla, we've got to get you home to your aunt."

Her face relaxed, and her eyes sparkled. "You mean you're coming with me?"

"No, angel. But I'll get you on the right train."

She looked so dejected that he quickly added, "We'll ride together to Friedrichstrasse. That's a whole half hour that we still have together!"

Only half an hour, she thought, suddenly aware of her surroundings, of the city square, the buildings, the ruins, the antiaircraft gun at the corner, and the people rushing past. To her dismay, Rolf was already leading the way into the crowd of hundreds of people that streamed toward the station. She hurried after him, calling, "Rolf! Rolf! What about my bike? Can we take my bike?"

He didn't even turn when he answered, "Sure. We have special cars for bikes, baby carriages, and invalids. Wait over there! I'll get the tickets."

Over there. Over where? She was being shoved and kicked, pushed and swept along by the crowd, like a twig in a stream. She craned her neck, looking for Rolf, tried to see above or at least past all those rushing people. She was afraid of getting crushed, almost screamed, but then she spotted that wonderful, silly grin—right in front of her.

"Scared?" He yelled over the din. "Might as well get used to it if you want to become a Berliner! Here's your ticket.

Hold onto it and follow me," he said as he shouldered the bike.

She had not believed it possible that it could get more crowded, that yet more people could fit into the small space. But they could. All those coming to the station were now funneled up the confined space of the staircase that led to the platform. Halfway up, she heard the train come in. Everyone heard it. Heads were pulled between shoulders, and the crowd, as if seized by madness, lurched forward. Elbows rammed sides; briefcases became weapons, ruthlessly slamming into legs and backs. A stampede of gigantic proportions propelled Tilla past Rolf toward the platform entrance. Tilla, like someone about to drown, lunged for the center post, clung to it until Rolf came into view. Only when she had a solid grip on the bike did she let go of the post.

She remembered the Berlin trains from her only visit to Aunt Liz. They had made a great impression on her. They were so nice and very fast, also a bit scary with their pneumatically closing doors. She had looked forward to riding them again. But this was different. There were so many people she couldn't even see the train!

The crowd pushed relentlessly, asserted tremendous pressure, and suddenly they were aboard, packed in solidly. She was painfully wedged against her bike, pedal biting into her calf, and certain no one else could get on. But those outside took aim. Like a trained team of stevedores, they pushed in rhythm. *Hau-ruck! Hau-ruck!* Those inside were pressed together as another group got on. Barely, for they had to pull in their coats, even bags in order for the doors to close. But close they did. The solid wall of people still left on the platform reluctantly stepped back when the train began to move.

The train, on its way to the center of town, sped through acres of ruins. Miraculously, many houses were still standing, and there were normal-looking streets left in this wasteland of charred, gutted buildings, twisted girders, mountains of rubble.

Most of the men and women on the train looked shabby and tired, as they rocked with the staccato rhythm of the train. Tilla looked at Rolf, but he was looking somewhere else. Following his glance, she saw a beautiful young woman, elegant hat rakishly set on black curls, answering his smile with a broad one of her own.

For the first time Tilla considered how she must look, with her dumb pigtails, coat made out of an army blanket, ripped pants. It didn't help at all that Rolf, turning back, said into her ear, "Gorgeous, isn't she? Someone to dream about!"

She had wanted him to dream of her. That had been childish, obviously. Even when she grew up, she knew she'd never look like that. Much to her relief, the beauty got off at the next stop. But before getting lost in the crowd, she had managed to direct another smile at Rolf.

Rolf. Rolf. Rolf. Soon she would be without him, alone— but, yes, with Aunt Liz. Would he write? Maybe they should arrange to meet at a certain place and time? She wanted to ask him, didn't know how. Every sentence that came to her head seemed more stupid, improper, and demeaning than the one before. She ended up by saying, "Hermsdorf. Schlosstrasse Seven, that's where I'll live. Maybe I should write it down?"

Apparently that was foolish, too, since he replied, "I know. I'll remember. Don't worry, I'll remember."

The macabre sight of the ruined city disappeared as the train went underground. Lights went on, sparse blue lights, which cast a ghoulish sheen on everyone.

"Potzdamer Platz," the loudspeakers blared as they pulled into a station, and passengers pressed toward the doors.

"We're not getting off here. Ours is the next stop," Rolf said. But they were being forced out, anyway, because they were in the way of those waiting to disembark. Rolf and Tilla were pushed against the people waiting outside. Nobody gave an inch. Tilla had visions of being caught between the people getting off and those wanting to get on.

As the stream of those leaving the train turned into a trickle, the mass outside moved as one. The few stragglers, arms flailing, had to fight their way out and through the onrushing crowd.

Just as she had been pushed out, without any effort of her own, Tilla was now pushed back on. Surrounded by strangers and shoved ever farther inside. She had hardly room to breathe and none to turn around to look for Rolf. She finally managed to just at the moment when the loudspeakers blared, "All aboard! Step back from the tracks!" and the doors closed. Rolf was left outside, in the crowd still on the platform. She saw his face for but one second. In the next, Rolf, crowd, and station were gone. The train accelerated and moved through the underground caverns of Berlin toward the next station.

"Friedrichstrasse! Station is Friedrichstrasse!" The train disgorged its passengers. Tilla saw the mass of humanity pressing in on all sides, strangers threatening to crush her. She had a moment of extraordinary clarity, then her brain recoiled and refused to accept reality.

In normal times Tilla beating her fists against a steel pillar and screaming, "Mama, Mama," would have caused a commotion. But this was wartime. Chaos reigned as an air raid drove more and more people from the street down to the already overcrowded underground station, and she became just another obstacle in their path.

She was merely whimpering, muttering, "Hermsdorf, Schlosstrasse Seven," when, hours later, the stationmaster had noticed her and put her on the right train.

16

Hermsdorf showed few outward signs of the war. It was one of the lucky Berlin suburbs that had so far been spared from heavy bombardment.

The apartment building at Schlosstrasse 7 was as intact as most other buildings there. No shrapnel holes marred the façade, and the ornate stucco garlands which adorned the balconies had not lost a single leaf. The house looked the same as it had in 1910, when it was built. The store, too, had been there from the beginning. Stationery— F. Puckarski. Same sign, same owners. F. Puckarski was long dead, of course. But his son had taken over, and then his son's wife, Paula, after he was drafted. Paper Paula, her customers affectionately called her.

Paula, at forty, had the cheerful disposition of a young girl and the attractive looks which stem from good health and a loving heart. Men and women who shopped in her store enjoyed lingering there, glad to partake of her good humor. Especially now, during these dreary and frightening times.

There were no customers at four-twenty in the afternoon when Paula saw the girl with the bike. It had started to sleet, and the girl looked wet and unkempt. Her hair, though braided into pigtails, looked as if it hadn't been combed in a long time. Her coat was muddy, and her slacks were ripped and dirty. She carried a curious old canvas shoulder bag and had another bag hanging on the handlebar. Paula watched her as she carefully leaned the bike against the building and slowly, hesitantly opened the door. She looked greatly distressed. Her eyelids were red and swollen, and the gray eyes wandered, unable to stay on one spot.

Paula made her come in. She sat her by the potbellied stove and gave her a cup of hot cocoa, saved for a special occasion. The girl was incoherent, but Paula gradually found out that her name was Tilla. Tilla seemed to have lost her aunt Liz and was now searching for her brother Rolf or Rudi, Paula wasn't sure which, and she had asked,

"Where is Rufus?" *Heaven only knows what she's been through*, Paula thought, wishing that she could help. Obviously she was looking for a relative. "Tilla?" she asked softly. "Maybe you have an address?"

"Dresden, Rathausstrasse Ten A," came the prompt answer.

Paula tried to hide her shock. Could it be, was it possible that this girl had survived the terrible raid on Dresden? It would account for the state she was in. That was six days ago. Could she have biked all the way to Berlin? The more Paula thought about it, the more probable it seemed. She must have had a compelling reason to come here. "You are in Berlin now, Tilla. Do you know that?"

The girl stared into space, then slowly shook her head. Paula watched her, would have liked just to gather her into her arms and assure her that all would be well. Paula decided to try again. "You don't know that you are in Berlin?" The girl only shook her head. "Maybe you remember an address, Tilla. One that starts with Berlin-Hermsdorf?"

"Schlosstrasse Seven," Tilla said in monotone.

"But that's where you are." Paula wanted to shout but controlled her voice. There was no response from the girl. So she said it again. "That's where you are. Who lives here?"

"My aunt Liz. But I lost her! I lost her!" the girl whimpered, and then sobbed uncontrollably. All Paula could do was stroke that wet little head while her mind frantically went through the list of tenants. Liz? Liz? She thought of Ahlers. No, that was Herta. Then there was Grete Ober, Mrs. Grabetz? Liz Grabetz, she tried. *No, it's Vera*. Who

71

else? Mrs. Feuerlicht? Maybe? Liz Feuerlicht didn't sound right. But then how would she know? Mrs. Feuerlicht was Mrs. Feuerlicht. As far as she and everyone else in the house were concerned, she didn't have a first name. *Haven't seen her in months,* Paula thought. Then it struck her. Of course. It had to be Elizabeth Hoffart, and she knew why it hadn't occurred to her before. When she had met her many, many years ago, Mrs. Hoffart had made it clear that she detested Liz and wished to be called Elizabeth.

"Lousy weather," said the burly man coming into the store.

"Lousy weather, lousy times, Mr. Ahlers," Paula said, getting behind the counter, and, noticing his curiosity, shook her head to indicate that he shouldn't ask about the crying girl. He took the cue, made his purchases, and departed, a questioning expression still on his face.

Elizabeth Hoffart of all people, Paula thought with dismay, cold, fastidious Elizabeth. Paula was so wrapped up in her thoughts that it startled her suddenly to see Tilla standing in front of the counter, saying, "I have two-mark-fifty. Can I get some paper and colored pencils for that?"

"Of course," Paula answered, and put a selection before her. *Should I tell her now that I know her aunt?* she wondered.

The girl had stopped crying but seemed far away as she carefully selected a small pad and a few pencils. She made no attempt to pay, but moved like a sleepwalker toward the stove, sat down, and as pad and pencils fell to the floor, she wailed, "I'm so cold! Mama! Mama! I'm so cold!"

She did not resist when Paula led her next door to her apartment. She helped her out of her clothes, quickly discarded the idea of offering her a bath—first things first—and put the shivering girl under two down comforters. By the time she tucked the hot-water bottle in Tilla was asleep.

Since it was only five o'clock, and Elizabeth wouldn't return from work until seven-thirty, Paula spent the next two and a half hours running back and forth between her store and the apartment. She wanted to be there to comfort her should she wake up. Poor thing. And how, she wondered, would Elizabeth react if indeed it were her niece?

Elizabeth Hoffart walked briskly home, luxuriously protected against the icy wind by her big fur coat. In her mind she was already stretched out on the couch, listening to one of her favorite records. She would make herself a cup of *real* coffee (bought at black-market prices) and have a cigarette or two. Those were the best hours, at home in her beautiful apartment. She needed this, after the ruins and misery, the dirty, ragged refugees, and bombed-out people she encountered every day. God! How can they stand it? Her mind refused even to consider the possibility that it might happen to her. Yes, she'd spend a cozy evening with, maybe, one of Lehar's operettas. Tomorrow was Tuesday—or bridge evening. It was Elsa's turn, so she'd go over there to play cards. Wednesday she'd do her mending, as always. Thursday was her night to improve her English. Twenty new words a week. It would come in handy if the Western

73

Allies got to Berlin first, as she fervently hoped. Friday night was reading night, and Saturdays she usually had dinner at the Walters. Considering all, she managed to keep her life orderly. That was the way she liked it, and she would never understand how people could live in confusion. The idea of not knowing where a pair of scissors were when you needed them was thoroughly appalling to her.

She looked at the sky, but it was so dark that she couldn't see much. *Maybe with this weather there won't be an alarm tonight. Maybe I can risk spending one night in privacy, in my own comfortable bed.* She discarded that thought. It would mean bringing all her bedding upstairs. Too much bother. And there'd probably be an alarm anyway. The air-raid shelter for Schlosstrasse 7 was simply the cellar. Each tenant had a corner there and had "furnished" it as comfortably as possible. Nowadays almost everyone went to sleep there. It saved one from running up and down between the all clear and alarm. When you went to sleep in the cellar, you could, theoretically, sleep right through bombardment, alarm, and everything else. Very few people managed that. Those who did had nerves of steel, which she unfortunately did not possess. She had heart palpitations every time the sirens went off. Well, she'd have an hour or two in private comfort before going to the cellar. She smiled in anticipation and entered the foyer.

Paula shot out of her apartment to meet her. "Your niece Tilla is here!" Paula told her excitedly. "She's come all the way from Dresden on her bike!"

"My niece?" Elizabeth said in disbelief. "But I don't have a niece Tilla. My niece was called Renate, and I'm sure she's—"

"This girl was looking for her aunt Liz at this address," Paula interrupted her. "I thought it might be you since I don't know of another Liz or Elizabeth in this house. She's about fourteen and lived on Rathausstrasse in Dresden."

Elizabeth steadied herself on the banister. Her brother's daughter had survived the air raid—and she, Elizabeth Hoffart, would be expected to take her in. That, of course, was what one did. Suddenly she understood why kings of old beheaded the bearer of bad news. A wave of resentment against Paula swept over her. As if it were Paula's fault that her brother had left her a niece, that she now would be saddled with the girl. Her life was being intruded on, everything would be upset—and there was no way out. She briefly thought of orphanages. She didn't have enough room. Where would the girl sleep? *Not in* my *bedroom*, she thought, and certainly not in the balcony room. Academic questions. She'd have to make room in her corner of the cellar. She'd have to take her in, or people would look upon her as a monster. A monster, when she prided herself on her propriety, in always doing the right thing! There was no way out. *Heaven knows what kind of brat she is by now.* Cute enough the last time she had seen her. But Lisa, her sister-in-law, had been much too lenient. No discipline at all. Elizabeth sighed, heard Paula say, "If you don't mind, I really think we should let her sleep now. . . ."

75

"Yes, of course." Elizabeth was glad for any postponement and ready to go upstairs and make herself that cup of coffee. She really needed it now.

But Paula asked, "Don't you want to see her? She's going to be very pretty. But we'll have to be quiet, so she doesn't wake up."

Elizabeth did feel pity when she saw that tearstained, sad face. But pretty? Well, Paula, typically, was trying to be nice. They tiptoed out, and Elizabeth surprised herself by saying, "Poor Renate. It is her, and who knows what she's been through? I won't be able to replace her mother, but I'm going to try."

"I know you will," Paula said, but thought: *I hope so. I only hope so.*

"Shall I take her suitcase and things upstairs?"

Paula looked aghast. "Suitcase? She had nothing but the clothes on her back and her bike. I've already put it in the cellar. Can you imagine, a young girl biking alone from Dresden to Berlin?" She paused. "Elizabeth, you'll have to be very, very patient with her because—"

Paula instantly was sorry for that remark as Elizabeth snapped, "What makes you think I wouldn't be . . .?"

"Well, it's just, I think that she's in shock and her mind is a bit confused right now. . . ."

"That's hardly surprising, is it? We'll see when she wakes up. I'll just run upstairs and eat something. I'll be right down after that. All right?"

"Take your time. I will be here." Paula went back in and sat down sadly next to the sleeping Tilla.

Elizabeth went upstairs, thinking: *No clothes, where am I going to get clothes? And then ration cards—I'll have to go to town hall and get them. Why me? Why does this have to happen to me?*

17

Tuesday follows Monday, after February comes March—and then it's April. This was so even in 1945, the last year of the terrible war.

On April 5 thousands of Allied planes made yet another large-scale attack on Berlin. People hiding in cellars had every reason to think that the end of the world had come. Tons and tons of bombs dropped out of the sky with infernal howling and screeching. Ruins, burned out but still erect, were hit for the fourth and fifth time. Earth erupted as they crumbled to the ground, and chunks of plaster and brick were hurled into the crater-riddled avenues. Garden walls and lampposts, statues and houses—everything seemed to explode.

In the center of this inferno, but forty feet belowground, Adolf Hitler, responsible for it all, took his place at the head of the conference table. SS officers, immaculately dressed in splendid uniforms and boots polished to a high gloss, greeted the generals he had summoned. Oriental carpets softened their steps. Talk and the clinking of brandy glasses were the other noises in the Fuehrer's bunker, while above, all hell was breaking loose. Only three years ago Europe had belonged to Adolf Hitler, from the Atlantic to the Volga. Now his Reich measured a mere 35 miles to the east and hardly more than 100 to the north, west, and south. The Allied and Russian armies were advancing from all directions. Soon his Third Reich would be a thing of the past. But he still talked of *victory*, and his sycophants nodded eagerly. Shielded from reality by the thick walls of his bunker and the yea-saying followers, he now gave orders that would, needlessly, kill thousands and thousands more.

Rolf Severin had every intention of staying alive. Admittedly, at this moment his chances didn't look very good. God knows he had a good enough view from the very top of the zoo bunker, where he was forced to feed one of the two monster antiaircraft guns. He could see it all too clearly —the falling bombs and where they hit, the fires and explosions below, as well as the enemy planes overhead. *I'm right in the middle of all this shit*, he thought, *protected by nothing more than a steel helmet.*

A red-hot piece of shrapnel whistled past, missing his arm by a mere quarter inch. Noticing that the gun was about to be fired again, he instinctively clapped his hands over his ears to muffle the deafening, ear-splitting sound. At that moment he received so solid a kick to his rear end that he wanted to scream. He could have. No one would have heard him as he didn't hear the officer he now faced. His mouth shaped a word. Rolf couldn't hear, but the message was clear enough. MOVE! MOVE the ammunition! MOVE the empty shells out of the way! MOVE your ass!

Rolf moved. The blisters on his hands were becoming calluses. Every bone in his body ached, and to top it all, his helmet, because it was much too large, insisted on doing a constant dance on his head. He didn't know what day it was, couldn't remember how long he'd been doing this. But he'd never forget or forgive those bullies who had gotten him here. One day he'd find them and get even. Just to think about them made his blood boil in frustrated fury, as he told himself for the umpteenth time that there had been *no way in the world* to get back on that train . . . and for him, there had not been another. Those two Hitler Youth bullies had come and marched him to this post.

The constant clanking of the munitions elevator suddenly stopped—one sweet moment to straighten up and rest. *Tilla*, he thought, *my poor Tillangel*, as he looked north toward Hermsdorf, where the low clouds seemed to be as much on fire as the buildings themselves.

"Crew change!" someone yelled as a new group of soldiers and Hitler Youth appeared. Rolf followed his own weary group through the metal hatch, down the concrete stairs, into the interior of the bunker.

They were too exhausted to bother with anything but getting their bodies into horizontal positions. The boys flopped down on the available bunks or simply on the concrete floor and were asleep instantly. The whole lot of them. Still in their uniforms, they lay helter-skelter, curled up, stretched out. Even those who had bedrolls had been too tired to undo and use them.

First Lieutenant Marantz surveyed this scene and absent-mindedly scratched the three-day-old stubble on his cheek. He hadn't had much sleep and no chance to shave or clean up since he had received the order. The stench in this crammed bunker compartment, a mixture of sweat, urine and excrement, and God knows what all, was so sickening he tried to do without breathing. That and the intolerable noise. *How the hell*, he wondered, *can these guys sleep here?* He looked down on this ragtag group of dirty, emaciated boys in torn and filthy uniforms. For a second he had the urge to put them all properly to bed and tuck them in, one by one. Ridiculous, of course. His order was clear. He knew what he had to do.

Colonel General Gotthard Heinrici, or so the rumor went, had told the Fuehrer bluntly that he didn't know how long his troops could stave off the Russians once they had begun their attack on Berlin. Adolf Hitler had flown into a rage and told him to use reserves. Heinrici then had had the gall to tell the Fuehrer that there was no such thing as a reserve army anymore. The leader of the Hitler Youth, Artur Ax-mann, had then suggested that his boys would become the new reserve. He pledged they would fight like men. Hitler had liked that and issued the order.

Lieutenant Marantz didn't know whether all this was true. But he knew that he had been ordered to collect every Hitler Youth he could find and immediately, and in any way possible, get these boys to the eastern front. There, he'd been told, they would get weapons and training in how to use them.

He had thought it was a good idea when he clicked his heels and saluted his commander with a *Heil Hitler.* A lot of these boys were strong and eager to prove themselves men. What better chance to prove your manhood than by defending the fatherland? They would certainly be more valuable troops than the old men who were now being drafted into the Home Guard. It had sounded good. But now, as he looked at this group of sleeping, worn-out boys, it seemed ridiculous. Still duty was duty, an order still an order. He knew of no alternatives—and the truck was waiting.

"UP!" he screamed as loud as he could, to be heard over all the other noises. "UP! UP! UP! IN LINE AND AT ATTENTION!" There was scarcely a movement. A few of the boys blinked unbelievingly. "UP! THIS IS AN ORDER! ARE YOU DEAF, YOU SONS OF BITCHES? WHAT KIND OF PITIFUL PIGSTY IS THIS HERE ANYWAY?" Marantz kicked the boy closest to him and yelled at the top of his lungs, "IN LINE—AND COUNT THROUGH! ON THE DOUBLE!"

Sleepy and hollow-eyed, the boys scrambled to do as they were told. The tallest one still ambled, unsure where to stand. Marantz hit him in the face. By the time the boy's cheek turned red they were in line and counting.

A dozen. That with the forty already on the truck made fifty-two. A full load. "DOWNSTAIRS—IN SINGLE FILE!" Lieutenant Marantz bellowed. As they filed past him, he read their belt buckles. The message, he knew, was on his own. *Gott mit Uns! "Gott mit Uns,"* he repeated in his mind but couldn't help adding, *I hope so, I sure hope God is with us,* as he led his troop down to the street.

18

Crafty Sergeant Max believed less in God than in preparation. "Every man for himself, God for us all," was his motto. Many a bag of the cement he trucked had found its way to his own home. He had reinforced his cellar walls until they were three feet thick. Heavy steel girders, exchanged for cement, held up the equally strong ceiling. His own private bunker would protect him against whatever planes might drop or guns might fire.

"Ida," he had boasted to his wife, "this thing can take a direct hit, and we'll still be all right." He had almost hoped for a bomb to fall on it—a small one, mind you—just to prove how strong it was.

Yeah! And a hell of a lot of good it does me right now, he thought as he steered his truck through the ruined wasteland of the city. He lit a cigarette and sang, "If there's fire in the house, Minimax will put it out," and added his own two lines to the advertising ditty, "But if you're out and on a fling, Minimax won't do a thing."

"Ain't exactly a fling going to Strausberg," he said aloud, and veered sharply to avoid a huge lump of concrete lying in the middle of the highway. He tried to keep his eyes on the road, but the horizon was of far greater interest. He knew those puffs of smoke too well. They were the visual accompaniment to the constant rumble of the frontline guns. Battlefront in Strausberg, outskirts of Berlin. *For all I know the Russki's already there.*

He had a load of barbed wire, Bruno spirals they called them, had been ordered to take it to the Third Army Group —second line of defense supposedly. Barbed-wire spirals to hold the Russians at bay? Laughable! Fortress Berlin, he sneered. What bunk! He got around and knew better than most that Berlin was undefendable, that the German military had never made provisions for what was happening now.

Stay alert, Max. Keep your eyes and ears open, he told himself, *sniff the situation and drop the load at the first opportune moment.* After that, nothing but home to Mother.

ZZZZZSSSSS-VOOoommm . . . ZZZzzzzsss-VOooommmmm! Artillery! *Damn! Too damn close! How the heck did I get so damned close?* He gunned the engine, turned the next corner, and quickly came to a stop. One look at the scene was enough. "Shit!" he said with feeling as he shut off the engine.

19

"Shit!" said Paula when she heard the hoarse rattling that always preceded the full-volume howl of the sirens. Paula rarely cursed, but this was one of the occasions that warranted a word like this. Tilla had been standing in line for three hours. If it weren't her turn right now, she'd come home without bread. She was supposed to come home the moment the sirens went off. "Oh, shit!" Paula screamed along with the sirens, giving full alarm. *We haven't had any bread for three days. If she comes home without it, we won't have any for who knows how long.*

She locked the store and anxiously looked in the direction of the bakery, where a large crowd waited in line. She couldn't see Tilla, and no one seemed to budge. It took more than a wailing siren for hungry, battle-hardened Berliners to give up their places. A hell of a lot more would have to happen.

Paula shielded her eyes against the sun. Since she still couldn't see Tilla, she decided to go get her. Walking along the edge of the small park, she was surprised to see the trees green with young leaves. It would, could be a beautiful spring day if it weren't for the war. She looked up when she heard the familiar hum of planes. *There's no antiaircraft-gun fire,* she thought. *They must be ours.* She watched the planes—V formation after V formation of sparkling silver planes—so many that they filled the sky and the ground began to vibrate in rhythm with their engines. She watched, spellbound, and couldn't believe her eyes. It couldn't be!

They were tiny dots at first—millions and trillions of gray dots, like large snowflakes. There were so many that they darkened the sky. Bombs! For the first time in all these years Paula actually *saw* bombs falling. Gray metal barrels with pointed noses and tailfins came toward her, down on her. They weren't big, but there were many, many, many . . .

She saw Tilla, for an instant, as they were running toward each other, and then . . .

Giant crescendo! Explosions, screaming, shooting all blended into one, one hellish, indescribable, torturous, end-of-the-world noise!

Paula had been thrown to the ground, was now flung up into the air, then dropped again. Earth acted like a springboard as she was lifted and dropped, lifted and dropped, until what felt like a ton of earth was dumped on her, pinned her down, and everything turned black.

She was sure that she was dead until she felt a desperate desire to breathe and couldn't. She wanted to scream, but her mouth was full of sand. Buried alive! *I'm buried alive,* she thought, and began digging and kicking in panic. She dug with her bare hands, kicked, tried to move out of this darkness, and didn't even know in which direction. Finally, as she clutched and pulled on a clump of grass, her head came clear. She lay still, spit out the sand, and inhaled. *I'm alive! I'm still alive,* she thought in amazement. How long had she been buried? For how long had the bombs come down? She didn't know, couldn't have said. But she knew that the noise had stopped. All was quiet—an eerie quiet. She lay there numb, tentatively moved first one leg, then the other. They functioned; so did her arms. She opened her eyes, saw each leaf of the bright green young grass, saw an ant run back and forth in panic. *You and me both,* she thought. Looking past the ant, she found herself staring into a pair of wide-open gray eyes.

"Tilla! Tilla! Tilla!" she screamed as she scrambled to her feet. Tilla blinked and then got up slowly.

"You're alive! Thank God you're alive!" Paula cried, embracing her. She felt tears streaming down her face. As she hugged the trembling Tilla, she silently prayed, *Please, God! Don't let her go into shock again. She was just beginning to function. . . ."*

"I did get the bread, Aunt Paula," Tilla said, prompting another outburst of tears from Paula. Tears of gratitude. She was about to hug Tilla again when she saw that the bottom loaf in the shopping net was bloody, bloody from Tilla's leg, which was bleeding profusely.

"You're hurt! You've been hit!" Paula cried in alarm. "We have to get you to a doctor!"

Tilla looked at her leg in surprise. "It doesn't hurt," she said, "really it doesn't," as she limped toward the house.

Fire engines and an ambulance sounded their horns noisily as they passed by. Paula sighed with relief when she saw that Schlosstrasse 7 was still there. But in front of her store, at the spot where she had stood, was a huge hole—first of a neat row of bomb craters, each five to six feet in diameter, which crossed the park and went all the way to the bakery.

86

There were second and third rows, trees were missing, cut off, uprooted, and the house with the bakery was burning.

"It's not as bad as it looked," Elizabeth told Inge, the secretary she shared her office with. "It's only a flesh wound. Unfortunately it bled so hard I had to cut up an old sheet." She sighed. "Can't even get bandages—that on top of everything else."

They listened to the distant rumble, anxiously looked at each other for a moment. "Russian artillery! It's getting closer," Inge said as she stapled two letters together. She shrugged. "Ah! What can you do? We have to take what comes. But," she continued, "I would have thought that it might bring her out of it. You know, another shock to get rid of the first one."

"She isn't actually in shock anymore," Elizabeth said. "I mean she functions. It's just that she's still withdrawn. Doesn't cry, doesn't smile. She just sits and stares holes into space."

"At least she doesn't give you any trouble," Inge said. "Some kids are so cocky and brash you feel like smacking them one."

"I know," Elizabeth agreed, "but when you get no reaction whatsoever, that also can drive you crazy. When she got the coat and dresses, I thought there might be a little smile, some sign of joy. Nothing at all. I gave up my perfectly good camel's hair coat and that gray wool dress you know, the one with the big collar?"

"I liked that one," Inge said.

"I did, too. And it matches the color of her eyes perfectly, so I thought it would please her. How many people would do that? Not many, right? And do you know what I had to pay the seamstress? Thirty mark each for the dresses, fifty-five for the coat. That should be enough—but not for Vera Grabetz. She's the one in my house. She had the gall to insist on half a pound of real coffee. She made it clear she knew I had a source."

"I'll see if I can get you some more!" Inge interjected.

"Well, anyway, she does look nice, especially in the coat. No one can say that I don't care for her."

"You mean she put those beautiful clothes on and said nothing?"

" 'Thank you, Aunt Liz.' That's what she said. Stoneface Renate . . . and I have to call her Tilla, silly name, but she insists on it. Talks in the monotone of an automaton. Put a nickel in, and it says, 'Thank you, Aunt Liz.' Aunt Liz! How I hate that! I've told her time and again that my name is Elizabeth, but I might as well talk to a wall. Makes no difference. She keeps saying 'Aunt Liz.' " Elizabeth sighed. "I've given up. And right now that's the least of my worries."

"You say she's fifteen? What does she do all day?"

"She stays with Paula, the woman who owns the stationery store. Paula says that even she sometimes forgets that Tilla is there. Sits by the stove. Sometimes she draws. Paula says she has talent. I can't see it. A boy in a Hitler Youth uniform with a pack, that's the only thing she draws."

"Better make sure the Russians don't see that!" Inge said,

then hesitated before she went on. "Have you thought of putting her into a home? I mean," she added hastily, "there are special institutions where they know how to deal with kids like that."

"She's not an idiot!" Elizabeth said sharply.

"I didn't say that," Inge countered, "but there are places where they have doctors who might know how to get her out of her lethargy or apathy or whatever it is."

"I have thought about it," Elizabeth now admitted, "but it's impossible right now. You know that. All the hospitals and orphanages are overcrowded. They wouldn't take her, not as long as I have an apartment. And I don't think I could—" The ringing telephone interrupted her.

Inge picked it up. "Borsig Industries," she answered, as she had 100,000 times before, and then cried, "Oh, Mother! Oh, my God! Oh, *no!* What? What? I can't hear you!" The last was a great wail: "Mother!" She screamed again, "Where are you?" Apparently she could hear again. "Where are you?" She now sobbed. "Yes, yes, of course, I'll meet you there. I'll come as quickly as I can." She placed the receiver back on the hook, stared at Elizabeth, then sat down and buried her head in her hands.

"What is it? What's happened?" Elizabeth asked, and went to her. "Inge! What's happened?"

"They're in Strausberg already," Inge cried. "The Russians are in Strausberg, and they've shot my father. Oh, God! Why? Why? He was seventy last week, and these pigs shoot him!"

"The Russians shot your father?"

"No!" Inge wailed. "The SS. They drafted him into the Home Guard." Inge blew her nose and tried to control herself. Still crying, she went on in a very low voice. "Seventy years old, and they made him dig ditches. Mother said he came home when he saw the Russians at the end of their street, and then the SS came and dragged him out. They said he was a deserter, and they shot him." Big tears streaming down her face, she hammered her desk with her fists. "Those pigs shot him in front of his own house!"

"It's awful. I'm sorry, Inge. I'm sorry," Elizabeth muttered, not knowing what else to say.

Inge got up and went for her coat. "I've got to go. You'll talk to Mr. Schmit, won't you? Mother is at my sister's. I've got to get there. She says everything is disintegrating. Oh, God, I hope I'll get—"

The door of their office was flung open. Mr. Schmit stormed in, looked at the two women, and thundered, "You're sick! You're both *sick!* I can't tolerate sick people here! How can we win the war with people like you?"

Inge and Elizabeth looked at him uncomprehendingly, convinced that their normally soft-spoken and even-tempered boss had lost his mind.

"I order you to go home immediately!" he screamed, and his voice broke. "Go!" he squeaked. Then it came back to normal. "Go home!" he yelled and added, "Don't you dare come back until you're really well!"

Dumbfounded, both women stood as if rooted to the ground. He came toward them, and when he was close, he quickly looked over his shoulder before he whispered,

90

"Don't you understand? I'm sending you home because the Russians will be here any minute! It's time to make yourselves scarce! Go! Go home! While there's time!" And then he watched impatiently and in exasperation as they tidied up, covered their typewriters, closed file drawers, stacked mail in the out basket. *They can't help it,* he thought. *Force of habit. Even now they have to make order when in the next moment everything can be blown to smithereens.* "Go! For heaven's sake, go!" He tried to hurry them—and called softly after them, "Stay alive!"

Elizabeth wasn't far from home, only three stations on the electric commuter train. The train was overcrowded, but she did get on, and couldn't know how lucky she was.

She thought about the approaching Russians. What would it be like? The terrible stories of murder and rape were too numerous and detailed to be dismissed as rumors. Everyone had his own scheme for how to avoid the worst. Vera Grabetz was going to dirty her face and pretend to be old, ugly, and sick. Paula wasn't sure what she would do or rather where she would hide. Pastor Scheuermann's wife, the staunch Nazi who had been decorated with the "mother cross" for bearing six children, still believed in a miracle. Even last night, as Russian artillery shells exploded all around them and the fires of neighboring communities lit the sky, she had declared loudly that the Fuehrer would win the war. Elizabeth despised the slovenly woman but didn't think she'd be stupid enough to want to defend Schlosstrasse 7. *If she gets the SS and Hitler Youth to barricade themselves in our house . . . amen!* Elizabeth thought, and felt ice-cold fear crawl up her back and stomach. She thought of her hiding place, a small, hidden-behind-a-dresser closet that she would have to share with her niece. Saw it suddenly as a trap, a coffin from which they might not escape.

At this very moment a scene of ultimate horror was being played out in real life. An estimated 10,000 people, crammed into a railroad tunnel in the center of Berlin, were about to be drowned like rats by the action of a few of their countrymen.

The wounded of four hospital trains and a crowd that had sought shelter there from the shelling and bombs screamed, fought, pushed, and trampled one another in their vain struggle to get to higher ground and safety.

For the Nazi regime it was zero hour. True to the Fuehrer's order to leave the enemy nothing but "scorched earth," a few fanatical SS men had blown up the sluice gate separating tunnel from river. Only a few people got out as the waters of the Spree River rushed in.

When Elizabeth stepped off onto the Hermsdorf station platform, the crew abandoned the train. It had been the last one out of the city. On the adjacent track sat a freight train, the two locomotives still belching big clouds of smoke, but that crew, too, had left.

"Red Cross packages! It's full of Red Cross packages for American prisoners!" The awed whisper went from mouth to mouth, a murmur at first, but soon the soft, hissing sound became a battle cry. People jumped off the platform, scurried over the track, and stormed the train.

Elizabeth hesitated for only a moment before she took the three-foot jump. By the time her feet touched down a group of men had already opened one of the boxcars and begun to throw square packages into the waiting hands of the crowd. Elizabeth was caught in the frenzy, had to duck as the parcels came down, and still was hit on the head by one. Paying no attention to the pain, she reached for it, wrapped her arms around it, and used it as a battering ram to get out of the melee. She stumbled down the embankment and crawled under the fence which protected the railroad property, ripped her coat and stockings, but never once let go of the parcel.

Word of this windfall, the trainload from the land of milk and honey, had apparently spread rapidly. People were coming from all directions, with shopping nets and baskets, handcarts and wheelbarrows. Butcher Naumann even came with his truck. Like a swarm of locusts, the hungry Hermsdorfers descended on the train. They seemed oblivious to the fact that machine-gun fire and rifle shots now mixed with the continuous noise of artillery. When fighter planes came down on strafing runs, they ducked into doorways, but seconds later they were back on the street, drawn to the train as if by a giant magnet.

Elizabeth flattened herself against a wall when she saw a plane but was off and running the moment it had passed. She couldn't wait to drop her precious package at home and run back for another. She'd tell Paula and Vera, of course, thought of taking Tilla along, but quickly dismissed the idea. The images of butter, coffee, chocolate, cigarettes, sugar, ham drove her almost mad. For the first time in her life, Elizabeth didn't care how she looked. She was too pre-occupied to notice that she had just passed the first Russians, and though she looked in their direction, the Russian tanks lining up along the small park in front of Schlosstrasse 7 simply failed to register. She found a completely empty house.

Paula, Vera, Pastor Scheuermann's wife, the Ahlers, old Mr. Muffel, everyone was either already at the train or on his or her way there. Even Tilla was out in the street, despite her promise to Paula that she would stay home.

The three Russian officers in the jeep, their machine pistols at the ready, had expected fighting Germans. They were puzzled by the two distinct streams of people, one coming, all with identical packages, and the other, without packages, hurrying toward the station. Most puzzling to the Russians was the fact that no one took the slightest notice of them. People continued to rush by, even when they jumped off their jeep and stopped two women at gunpoint. Paula and Vera froze, didn't dare bat even an eyelash, watched in mortal fear as bayonets slashed through their packages.

It couldn't be! It was all unreal, the cigarettes and the coffee, the labeled cans as well as the Russians.

"All good now! Hitler *kaputt!*" one of the Russian officers said, smiling, and insisted on shaking Paula's fear-sweaty hand. Then the three officers leaped back on their jeep and left two stunned women standing there.

More and more Russians followed and merged with the

ever-increasing crowd. On foot, on bikes, on motorcycles, on horse-drawn wagons, they mingled with the trek of people to the station. Finally, because there were so many of them, the Germans noticed.

"The war is over!" someone shouted, and the cry was picked up by the crowd. "The war is over! The war is over! The Russians are here!"

As the Russians laughed and joined in the chorus, Germans, too, were beginning to smile and nudge one another. "Look, look!" they said in amazement. "They're people like us!" They embraced each other. Many wept as they shouted again and again, "The war is over!"

It didn't slow the rush toward those fantastic packages. Germans and Russians alike still moved toward the train, as fast as their legs or wheels would carry them. But every so often the happy crowd scattered in all directions when another barrage of artillery came screeching in and shells exploded nearby.

Tilla was walking in the middle of the street when a plane, machine guns blazing, began its descent. Out of nowhere a girl appeared and yanked her into a doorway as a neat row of bullet holes was stitched in the stones.

"You crazy or something?" the girl shouted over the shooting, without waiting for an answer. "Don't you know the war is over? The Nazis are gone! The war is over!" she sang out and danced Tilla around. Waving at the passing Russians, she screamed, "Long live the Red Army! Long live the victorious Red Army!"

"Tilla," she said in answer to the girl's "I'm Lotte," and

95

allowed herself to be dragged toward the train. But when she saw the looting mob there, she stopped and stubbornly refused to go any farther.

Lotte, a sturdy, dark-haired, handsome girl of Tilla's age, pulled on her arm with renewed vigor. "Come on!" she pleaded. "We've got to get some of those parcels! There's no food. The stores are all sold out or looted. The Russians have nothing themselves. How are we going to live?" she asked urgently. "Come on! Come on. I can't do it alone, but together we can," she said as she dragged the reluctant Tilla to the fringe of the frenzied crowd. "You're slim. You can get in there. Get in there," she ordered, "but watch for me. That's all you have to do. I'll climb on that one there." She pointed to one of the freight cars. "I'm good at that. Just watch and catch what I throw you!" Lotte was swallowed up by the crowd before Tilla could protest.

There was no choice. Tilla followed her, made her way, crawling, pushing, squeezing by, until she stood directly under the door. Lotte, true to her word, was up there, smiling at her, an "I told you so" smile. Tilla smiled back, reached up, and caught the first box. Lotte and the second box came down together.

At that moment all hell broke loose. Planes fired at the train, people screamed, shots rang out, and one of the freight cars burst into flames.

"I'll make a path!" Lotte yelled. "Follow me!" Tilla followed—through the crazy, raging crowd, down the embankment, under the fence, over another along a garden wall. Breathing heavily, they rested under a forsythia bush.

The street looked very different now. Russian tanks, their turrets turning, searching, slowly rattled along, followed by armored cars and soldiers on foot. Two Russians, rolling a huge wooden cable drum between them, were laying a wire along the other side of the wall. They did not see the two girls. All the people were gone—vanished. Here and there someone would dart out of a house, only to disappear quickly into another.

"What's going on?" Tilla whispered fearfully.

"I don't know!" Lotte murmured. "But I don't like it. Don't like it at all." She hesitated and, with her mouth close to Tilla's ear, asked, "Where do you live?"

"Number seven. Three houses down."

"We're in number five. You must be new here."

Tilla wanted to answer, but Lotte didn't let her. She said, "I don't like what I see on the street. We'd better go over the back fences. You'll just have to follow me again." Even in a whisper, Lotte's voice had authority.

Tilla crept along on all fours, sometimes on her belly, sometimes dashing a few yards to the shelter of a tree or shed. She followed Lotte, imitating her despite the heavy shooting. There were also new sounds: howling Russian guns, machine-gun fire, artillery, and occasionally blood-curdling screams. Impossible to say who was shooting at whom, who was screaming and why. There was no time to think, no time either for long good-byes. "See you," Lotte said as she pushed Tilla into the back entrance of number 7.

"Tilla!" It was exclamation, exasperation, and sigh of relief all in one. Elizabeth hugged her niece for the first time. "Upstairs! Run upstairs to the apartment!"

Outside, guttural Russian shouts and commands drew closer. They raced upstairs. Elizabeth opened the door with shaking fingers and, once they were inside, tried to lock it. There was no time. Heavy boots were already on the stairs. Elizabeth pushed Tilla into the dressing room, moved the dresser aside, revealing a small door, almost invisible since it was covered with the same wallpaper as the rest of the room. Tilla climbed into a space that had been designed to store suitcases. Her aunt kicked the precious packages in, then with great effort and haste squeezed in herself, pulled the dresser toward her, and closed the door from within.

It was dark, and they huddled in impossible positions, yet dared not move. Russians were already in the apartment. Something heavy crashed; glass broke; rifle butts banged on walls. There was laughter and fierce cursing. On the street there was the unending rattle of heavy tanks accompanied by the ghoulish howl of grenade launchers. Above this din rose the spine-chilling screams of women. It went on and on, day and night, night and day before it abated.

Elizabeth didn't make a sound, but Tilla, feeling her shake, knew that she was crying. Reaching for her, she stubbed her finger, then hit her head when she inadvertently tried to sit up. Gingerly groping, she found Elizabeth's head at last and leaned hers against it. "It's all right, Aunt Liz," she whispered. "Everything is going to be all right," she told her aunt because in her mind she saw the fish tank filled with the undulating shapes of exotic fish and her easel with a canvas leaning on it, and the skylight and Rolf's grand piano in the next room. Saw it all so clearly and knew, suddenly, that she would have it all. Knew then that she wanted to live. "Everything is going to be all right," she repeated. "The war is over, Aunt Liz."

20

"WE'LL NEVER CAPITULATE! WE'LL FIGHT TO FINAL VICTORY!" the corporal screamed. "I'LL TEACH YOU HOW TO FIGHT LIKE MEN—YOU SORRY LOT OF WET SACKS! I'M GOING TO GRIND YOUR ASSES, UNTIL YOU THINK IT'S EASTER, CHRISTMAS, AND NEW YEAR'S ALL ROLLED INTO ONE!"

Twenty years old and only recently promoted to corporal, Hans Raumann was swollen with pride. His dream had come true. He was leading his own platoon of sixty men. It didn't concern Raumann at all that the men were boys, the oldest only fifteen years old—they were his MEN!

He had drilled and marched them until they collapsed— marched them again, and again. They had dug trenches for twelve hours, after which Raumann had drilled them some more. Just to toughen them up. He taught them everything about rifles, though they did no actual shooting. To Raumann's chagrin, there was hardly enough ammunition for the real battle. He couldn't afford to waste it in training.

He had done his bit. His men were ready for battle when he marched them to the front on the outskirts of the capital, to fight the last big battle for Hitler's Germany. The battle for Berlin.

There was no way to escape pistol-brandishing Raumann and his zealous inner clique. The smallest kid in the group, little Heiner, had tried to "make himself scarce." He was brought back immediately and moments later hanged from a tree. Not long enough to die, but long enough to be an impressive lesson to all other members of "Battle Platoon Raumann." They would fight to final victory—or die, as ordered.

When Rolf Severin found himself under Raumann's command, he was sure that his luck had deserted him. On Raumann's orders he had marched until his feet wouldn't carry him one step farther, except that on Raumann's command they did. They had walked him right to the front, had miraculously held him up while he dug trenches, and against all odds, they had functioned well enough to allow him to advance, rifle in hand, behind one of the few remaining tanks. They had finally been given a rest in a small wood.

It was twilight, almost night, and before them stretched open fields, beyond which were the Russians. Rolf had been ordered, like the others, to dig himself a foxhole, from there to defend the fatherland and stem the Russian tide. "Every block, every house, every foxhole," the Fuehrer had declared, "have to be defended to the last breath!"

The Russians had attacked much sooner than anyone had expected. They advanced across the field, an avalanche of tanks, self-propelled guns, armored vehicles, and hundreds of thousands of screaming soldiers. The howling, inarticulate battle cry of attacking Russians almost drowned out the noise of the guns. Never before had Rolf felt so frightened and so alone.

Later he remembered one particular Russian coming toward him, his bayonet at the ready, remembered his own sweaty finger on the trigger of a rifle he had never fired. *I have to—I'm sorry, I have to—it's either you or me.* Did he shout it? Did he merely think it when he pulled the trigger? He'd never know because there was an enormous explosion at his ear and he received a shock that sent him backward into his hole.

The battle raged for hours. Russian tanks passed and retreated. Germans came, retreated, and advanced again. He cowered in his hole, surprised to be still alive.

Suddenly someone jumped on him and cursed—in German. The old Home Guard man and Rolf looked at each other in the first light of dawn. The old man breathlessly demanded to know what Rolf was doing in that hole; without waiting for Rolf's reply, he jumped out and dragged him along.

"Run, boy! Run as fast as you can! Run for your life!" the old man cried. And Rolf did. He ran through the woods, like everyone else, even the soldiers and Home Guard men, away from the battle. He ran until he thought his lungs would burst. Ran to get away from the shooting, until he was stopped by a brick wall. How he had climbed the wall he would never know. He remembered only that he fell down the other side. Dropped down like dead.

"Get 'em out of here! I order you to take them back this

minute. I am a soldier! I refuse to fight my battles with children!"

Rolf had heard the authoritative voice, the shouted orders, as if in a dream.

"Here's another one! Damm it!"

With that he had been lifted, thrown about. It didn't matter. Nothing mattered anymore.

When he came to, he lay fully dressed on a pile of straw. He sat up and looked around. He was in some kind of cellar on a straw-covered floor. There were about thirty men lying around, mainly old Home Guard and about a dozen wounded soldiers as well as a few Hitler Youths. He didn't know where he was or how he had gotten there, and he didn't care. Exhausted and incapable of thought, he lay down again and fell asleep.

The smell of food and clatter of tin mess kits had awakened him the second time. He lined up with the others at the huge kettle and received two ladles of soup from a smiling Red Cross nurse. Then someone heartily slapped him on the back, so heartily that half the soup jumped out of his kit. It was Raumann.

"Balm on my sore eyes to see you," the corporal said. "We'll show those Bolsheviks yet—right? Despite our losses, it's still victory or death! We're regrouping, so when you've finished eating, come next door. I'll work out your new battle station."

Rolf had stood thunderstruck. "You're doing a great job," said the nurse, and smiled at him. "You've got to hold out! Wenck's army is on the way. We'll win!" He allowed her to refill his mess kit, despite a sudden urge to ram her crazy, stupid head into the wall behind her.

Losses had been heavy indeed. Rolf found out that he was one of seventeen survivors from Raumann's original sixty. His new battle station was smack in the middle of the street, behind a barricade. A barricade that was an old streetcar. The defenders, Home Guard and Hitler Youth, had pushed it sideways so that it blocked the street, and then they had filled it with stones. On Raumann's orders, he was to stand behind it and fire on the advancing Russians. Raumann hoped to get a supply of bazookas. Rolf didn't. But with his luck they'd come, and Raumann would drill them in the use of those damn things. Rolf was sure that if he had to use one, he'd accidentally kill himself with it.

Here, in the center of Berlin, you couldn't even dig a hole. There was nowhere to hide because Raumann wanted to defend street, streetcar, and surrounding ruins to the last breath. *I've certainly landed in the biggest pile of shit*, Rolf thought miserably when an old truck turned the corner.

He looked at it dumbly. It seemed familiar, but he didn't know why until he saw the driver. Rolf rushed toward the truck but then was so overcome to see someone he knew that he couldn't think of anything to say. His small head almost disappearing under the large steel helmet, he looked up at Max and tried to grin.

Grubby, wrinkled Sergeant Max looked down at Rolf. His mouth widened in the beginning of a smile of recognition . . . and disappeared. Max turned abruptly away.

Max had recognized him . . . but— Rolf pulled his helmet as far down as it would go, and while the others unloaded the barbed wire, he pretended to inspect the tires, thus managing to hide his tears.

"You!" It sounded mean, but it was Max's voice and his hand that roughly grabbed Rolf by the collar. "Get in! We can't dawdle here! We've got work to do!" Max half lifted Rolf as he pushed him into the cab. "You're ordered to help me get the next load!" Max yelled as he slammed the door, revved up the engine, and started to back out.

Raumann, waving his arms wildly, came running and shouted, "Wait a minute! You can't do that! I need every man!"

Rounding the corner backward, at breakneck speed, Max leaned out of the window and shouted back, "You want your barbed wire, don't ya? I need help at the other end. We'll be back in no time!"

He turned the truck, already out of sight, and, wheels screaming, raced off, with the astonished Rolf beside him. "Wouldn't believe what the old girl still has in her," he said, grinning, and affectionately patted the steering wheel. Shoving his elbow into Rolf's ribs, he asked, "Surprised you, ha?" Rolf could only nod. "You look as if you've been through hell and back, kid," he went on, deftly avoiding a large bomb crater in the middle of the street, "or"—he gave Rolf a searching look—"maybe you'd rather have stayed there to final victory, ha?"

"Hell, *no!*" Rolf said. "It's just . . . I was so glad to see you, and then you seemed to know me and then you didn't. I couldn't understand what happened."

"You dumb or something?" Max asked. "Whatta you expect me to do? Maybe yell 'Hallelujah' and embrace you like my long-lost son? You know we'd both be there behind your barricade. The guy who ran after us, your com-man-der?" Rolf nodded. "Thought so, I know the type. And there's always been that little voice here"—he tapped his finger against his head—"that tells me, 'Max, stay away from guys like that.' The moment I turned the corner, I knew which hour had struck, I assure you! Max ain't stupid. In another hour or two our Russian friends are gonna make mincemeat outa the whole lot of these assholes, your little toy train notwithstanding. In situations like this, old Max knows only one motto and that's 'Home to Mother!' Hang on!" The truck swerved, first left, then right, as asphalt exploded. Debris rained on the truck, but it continued at breakneck speed. A roller-coaster ride over the churned up roads.

Max beamed as if he were enjoying himself tremendously. "Hungry?" He reached across Rolf and extracted an enormous ham sandwich from the indescribable mess of his glove compartment. "Eat, kid, eat. There's more where this came from. If we get there!" Rolf hesitated only for a second, then greedily bit into the sandwich. *"Shit!"* Max exclaimed as he shifted in such a hurry that Rolf thought the whole damn transmission would come apart. Instead, they suddenly moved backward and turned on two wheels. Rolf saw the Russian tank for just a moment; then they were safe behind a building, continuing in a slightly different direction. "Doesn't matter how you get there, right, kid"—

Max was laughing again—"as long as you get there? Good, ha?" He pointed to the empty sandwich paper. "Now you need something to wash it all down, and I'm fresh outa beer. Well, what the hell! Here." He reached under his seat and produced a bottle of vodka, which he handed Rolf. "*Na zdorov'e!* That's the toast from now on!" Rolf swallowed long and hard. He was feeling so good, giddily happy to have found Max, to be in the old stinking truck with him.

"Hey! Wait a minute!" Max took the bottle and, his eyes never leaving the road, drank a good third in one long gulp. He handed it back to Rolf, urging him, "Go on, we'll share. Say, what happened to your sister?"

"My sister?"

"That cute girl you were with when I picked you up in Sonnewalde."

"Oh!" said Rolf, grinning. "That wasn't my sister, that's my girl friend."

Max nudged Rolf with his elbow. "You rascal! And I let you sleep with her! Starting mighty early, aren't you?" He chuckled. "Aren't you the one to put one over on old Max. Well, what the hell—take your pleasures where and when you find 'em, ha?" He reached for the bottle again and took a long swig. They both laughed.

Max floored the gas pedal of the old truck when they passed burning buildings; but then he'd suddenly shift down, and they would crawl along, keeping intent eyes on tracer munition, falling shells, bombs. "Keep your eyes peeled! Keep your eyes peeled," Max hissed. At one point they saw a huge crowd waiting by a pump and watched in unbelieving horror as a bomb dropped right into the middle of it and earth and concrete, pails and people exploded into the air.

Then, as before, Rolf could only marvel at the way Max handled the truck and how it responded. They backed up, shot forward, crawled, or went like a bat out of hell. Whatever the situation demanded, Max and truck did it. And the vodka bottle passed between them—and they laughed.

A German lieutenant was standing on a rooftop, watching the scene through his binoculars. He focused on the careening truck, clearly saw the unshaved, unkempt sergeant behind the wheel, but was puzzled by a helmet which seemed to be floating next to the driver. It wasn't lying on the seat, yet there was no one visible under it either. He saw the boy just as the truck disappeared around a corner. A young boy with a pale, dirty face was under that big steel helmet. What struck the lieutenant as weird was that both driver and boy were laughing. He was sure that they had both been laughing. *Such a moment in history*, he thought, *and they laugh.*

They were almost through the second bottle of vodka when Max drove the truck into a garage. Whispering, "Be still, my heart," he emptied the gas tank, deflated the tires, threw a batch of old rags over the hood, and did all manner of other things before he patted the steering wheel once more, almost caressed it. "Good girl. Good old Rosinante, no one else will drive you. Max made sure. Don't worry, with a bit of luck, you and I'll be on the road again." He took Rolf's arm and walked him out through the back,

107

through a well-kept garden. "Time for a bit of shut-eye, don't you think?" The expression didn't bother Rolf this time; on the contrary he thought it funny and laughed, laughed even more when Max added, "Haven't listened to my mattress in ages!"

Max didn't have to open the door of the small bungalow type of house. His wife did. "H'lo, Mother!" said Max. "This here is . . ." He turned to Rolf. "What's your name?"

"Rolf."

"Yeah, right, Ruff," said Max. "My friend Ruff. See if you can't find him some other clothes. You know, something modern. Uniforms, I think, are fresh out of style."

The small woman looked at him, at Rolf, and back at Max. "*Drunk!* The Russians can be here any minute, and he comes home drunk! Comes home drunk and wants things. Clothes! Where am I gonna get clothes for a boy? Am I a magician?" She looked Rolf over. "Don't worry, we'll think of something. Well—don't just stand there, come on in."

What came next, happened very fast. Machine-guns ack-acked, rifle shots rang out, they heard Russian tanks rumble over the cobblestones, and then there were Russian voices. "Quick . . . they're here," Max's wife said. "The Russians are here."

They raced down a dark staircase to an ordinary cellar, from there into a strange concrete cubicle, and somewhere in between Max disappeared. Rolf wanted to ask, but the woman all but tore his clothes off him, until he stood in only undershorts and socks. She disappeared with everything he owned. Before he even knew what was happening, she was back. She forced him into a nightgown, tied a scarf around his head, and with amazing strength muscled him onto a cot, where she almost suffocated him with blankets. Then she hurried away again, returned with a small bottle, commanded him to hold still, while she dabbed drops of liquid over his face, then hers. The transformation on her was horrifying. She looked, with all those red blotches, like a carrier of a dread disease.

"They're scared of scarlet fever," she whispered, and as heavy Russian boots came down the stairs, accompanied by guttural voices, she began to wail, low at first, then louder. "Oh, my poor, sick child! My angel face! My poor, sick darling, oh, oh, oh!"

She kept it up while the Russians went over the house. They laughed as they searched the cellar, the bunker, and broke things, she moaned and wailed, "My poor, poor baby, my child," when they threatened her, only inserting, "No! *No! No!*" to their questions whether there were any soldiers in the house. A few had grabbed her, one had already wrestled her to the ground, but after one look at her face, he had dropped her in disgust.

It went on for hours. The shooting, though more distant now, continued, and the Russians kept coming. At times there were more than a dozen in the small bunker cubicle. And she never stopped wailing and moaning, but once muttered through her teeth, "Groan! You're in pain!"

At last they were alone. She sighed, wiped her brow with the end of her scarf, and quietly asked, "Whatta you think, will we make it big in the theater or won't we?" He spontaneously gave her a kiss, at which moment Max made his entry.

"This rascal! Now he's after my wife!" They were smiling, all three of them, though Rolf had a tough time recognizing Max. The sergeant, both legs in casts, hobbled around on crutches, dressed in a tattered shirt he seemed to have lived in for years and pants borrowed from a man at least twice his size. He looked twenty years older, and his bandaged hand was clearly deformed.

His wife, carefully checking every detail, nodded approval. Rolf wanted to applaud as well as question but was pushed back down on the cot.

"My baby! Oh, my poor baby," the wife wailed. Rolf closed his eyes, writhed, and sighed softly as if in great pain. He put his heart and soul into the performance. Max stumbled, dropped one of his crutches, cried out, then mumbled as if he were out of his mind. The next group of Russians had arrived.

21 Those were the last hours of Hitler's Third Reich. By now the Russians were occupying most of the devastated town. White sheets, the flags of surrender, were replacing those of the swastika. But fighting was still going on.

Miles of smoldering ruins, mountains of rubble where streets had been; crazily bent steel girders; the skeletal remains of buildings. Abandoned and burned vehicles, corpses of men and animals. What had been the city of Berlin was an apocalyptic panorama. Few people, however, except for the Russian pilots, had a chance at an overall view.

Edith Severin was one of them. She had only to get out from under her heavy oak dining table to look at the tableau of the burning city. Half the house had been blasted away during a bombing raid. The rest, including her third-floor apartment, was open to view like a dollhouse. Edith, so as not to be seen, existed in the few square feet behind the breakfront and under the table, her shelter from low-flying planes and shrapnel. Though high up, with nothing but the tabletop between her and the sky, she had trouble breathing because everything was covered with inches of dust, debris, and pieces of brick and concrete.

It was a miracle that she was still alive, and she wasn't sure that she wanted to be. What for? *Why not just step over the edge and be done with it?* crossed her mind more than once. She had fled to this precarious perch when a friend warned her of impending arrest and immediate court-martial. *Why did I climb up here? Why didn't I let myself be shot? They did it to Hans. The Nazis killed him in cold blood in Dachau concentration camp. Why not me, too?* And to believe, to hope that Rolf was still alive was only a mother's wishful thinking. She remembered taking

111

him to the train. Her only son, this frail little boy, one among many, on their way to an evacuation camp. He wore the uniform of those who had killed his father. Thinking he'd be safe, she had insisted that he join the Hitler Youth. *Safe,* she though bitterly. How stupid to hope that he would be safe. Hitler had promised to take care of those boys, Germany's future. She had not been able to find out from any of the Hitler Youth offices what had happened to the camp. She had heard rumors, though. One was that the camp had been overrun by the Russians and all the boys had been taken prisoners. The other one was equally horrifying. The train which was supposed to take them to safety had been bombed and all had been killed.

She had trouble digging through the different layers of clothing to get to the pocket where she kept Rolf's letter. The letter was dated November 10, 1944. Five long months ago. The young boys who were not missing were getting themselves killed in the streets down there. For what? For whom? Adolf Hitler?

She carefully peered around the edge of the breakfront and watched the Russians reposition their guns on the northern edge of the Tiergarten, then zero in on the Reich Chancellery, which was the big building next to the invisible Fuehrerbunker.

In one of the cellars of the bunker, a drunken orgy was in progress, a last desperate grasp on life by those whose power was coming to an end. In another, a doctor, who hadn't slept in days, operated on hundreds of wounded by

112

the dim light of a battery-powered lamp. He was wading in gore; because of the heavy shelling, his staff couldn't get outside to empty the containers that overflowed with amputated limbs.

In the Fuehrerbunker itself there was the smell of death. It was April 30, 1945. The Fuehrer was dead. He had shot himself with a Walther 7.65 pistol and simultaneously bitten on a poison capsule. Dead, too, was Eva Braun, the woman he had married only the day before. Loyal followers had carried their corpses outside, doused them with gasoline, and set them afire. They had not waited until the flames had consumed their Fuehrer's body but fled back into the relative safety of the bunker to avoid General Vasili Kasakov's artillery. But there were more corpses to dispose of.

Propaganda Minister Joseph Goebbels and his wife had also committed suicide. They, too, were carried outside. Those who attended to their "funeral" were by now short of gasoline and time; the Goebbelses' bodies were only charred.

Still in the Fuehrerbunker were the six small corpses of the Goebbels children. Their own mother had given them the poison. No one had the stomach to touch them.

Dead, too, was Blondi, the Fuehrer's pet dog, who had whelped only two months before. On her master's order she, too, had been poisoned.

For the remaining bunker inhabitants, generals among them, time was running out.

113

A day and a half later, on Wednesday 2, 1945, German generals Karl Weidling and Theodor von Dufving surrendered the city of Berlin to Russian Marshal Georgi K. Zhukov. Chief technician Johannes Hentschel was the only one left in the Fuehrerbunker to greet the Russians.

PART TWO

22 They were parched, faint from hunger and the smell, stench of their own making. Above all, it was the thirst, the overwhelming need for water, that drove Tilla and Elizabeth out of their hiding place. Blinded by the bright sun, Tilla staggered to the kitchen faucet. The pipe gurgled, and one drop of brown liquid came out . . . then nothing. Elizabeth had trudged to the bathroom. Stiff from the contorted position she had been in for so long, she had to support herself on the tub to turn the handles. She opened them all the way—nothing. She fell back, lay on the bathroom floor, moaning, "There is no water."

Later, when she remembered the pump in the yard, Tilla went down with a pail. Cautiously she stuck her head out the doorway, but there was no one in sight. She listened, but there was no sound. She dashed to the pump, greedily drank from her grimy hands, and splashed her face again and again, before she started to fill the pail. When she saw them, it was too late. The two scruffy Russians had already grabbed her, dragged her, screaming, toward the garden.

A short, sharp command stopped them. They turned to face the Russian officer without loosening their grip on her and laughed loudly. The officer seemed angry, he shouted, but her attackers laughed even more and excitedly talked back to him. Suddenly he whipped out his pistol and gesticulating wildly shot one, two, three shots into the air. The soldiers reluctantly released her and, grumbling, walked away.

The officer was very young and blond. His uniform tunic hung loosely around his broad shoulders, and a wide leather belt with holsters held it tight around the waist. Every feature of his face was classically perfect. There was about him an aura of healthy virility. He stamped his booted foot. "You should not be out!" he said angrily in perfect German, then commanded, "Show me where you live! Walk in front of me!" He waved her ahead with the still-smoking pistol.

Tilla knocked on the apartment door. When Elizabeth opened it and saw the Russian, only an unintelligible sound came out of her mouth. Tilla turned around and was surprised to see that the Russian had carried her pail, which he now set down.

"Captain Gorchakov," the officer said, then in a sharp tone asked Elizabeth, "Is this your daughter?"

"N-n-no," Elizabeth stammered. "My niece."

"You should know better! How could you allow her to go out?" Gorchakov snapped.

Elizabeth opened her mouth to protest, closed it when he made a quick motion with his hand as if to slap her. But he merely pushed her aside and walked into the apartment. He went from room to room, and when he came back, Elizabeth and Tilla were still standing where he had left them. "Clean up," he said, looking at Elizabeth. "I am going to lodge in the large room. I will—"

He never finished the sentence because there was suddenly a commotion downstairs. Russians seemed to be having a brawl, then a woman screamed, and from below old Mr. Muffel came panting.

"Officer, please!" he gasped. "Help! Quick! They're after Mrs. Feuerlicht!"

The captain, taking three steps at a time, was already rushing downstairs.

When Captain Gorchakov returned, he brought with him his army pack, a rather elegant leather suitcase, and Yuschka, his adjutant, a short Mongolian whose left arm was covered with watches from wrist to elbow. Yuschka handed Elizabeth an enormous chunk of dripping, bloody meat and, after fishing around in his trouser pockets, came up with a handful of potatoes. These, too, he gave to Elizabeth.

"I assume that you know how to cook, madam?" the captain said sarcastically, addressing Elizabeth. "I expect to dine in about two hours. You and your niece shall be my guests."

When Elizabeth pointed out that there was neither gas nor electricity he gave some orders to Yuschka. Yuschka left but soon returned, carrying Paula's potbellied stove, which he proudly dropped in the center of the kitchen. Elizabeth opened the gate to the firehole. It was empty. Yuschka looked into it, then around the kitchen. His face lit up, and before anyone had a chance to stop him, he had reduced one of the two kitchen chairs to firewood. Reprimanded in Russian by Gorchakov, he smiled sheepishly, then departed once more, to return with a sackful of coal and wood.

Captain Gorchakov uncorked the first of five bottles of vodka, handed Elizabeth a tumblerful, and, with Yuschka in tow, withdrew to the balcony room. Since the stove had no pipe, the kitchen was soon so full of smoke that Elizabeth and Tilla could barely see each other. But they battled valiantly to turn the revolting meat, of uncertain origin, into a meal. Finally, a frightened Elizabeth went to announce that dinner was ready. She stood in the doorway of her beloved balcony room, her heart beating so wildly that it echoed in her ears. She stared at the scene before her and couldn't believe her eyes.

"*Vous êtes étonnée, madame?*" Gorchakov asked.

She stood transfixed, unable to answer. Never in her life would she have expected what she now saw.

The captain had set her table for a banquet, using her damask cloth, her best china, her crystal glasses, silver flatware, and candlesticks. *He's gone through all my things,*

Elizabeth thought; *he's even found the candles I saved for so long.*

Captain Gorchakov smiled. *"Vous approuvez, madame?"*

During the extraordinary dinner that followed, Elizabeth had had to face Yuschka, the Mongolian. Tilla had been directed to sit opposite the captain. Gorchakov had been generous, too generous, with the vodka, always filling their glasses to the brim. Elizabeth and Tilla dared not refuse when he insisted that they observe Russian custom, which meant bottoms up after each toast. Gorchakov and Yuschka had toasted the esteemed Generalissimo Joseph Stalin, toasted the victorious Red Army and the great Supreme Commander of the Soviet Land Forces Marshal Vasili I. Chuikov and the victorious Marshal Georgi K. Zhukov and the end of Nazi terror and the peace-loving peoples of the great Soviet Union . . . and the peace-loving Germans . . . and toasted the friendship, everlasting, of the peace-loving peoples of the great Soviet Union and the peace-loving peoples of Germany and all other . . . Elizabeth swayed and would have fallen had the captain not caught her. He and Yuschka had carried her off to bed, then talked in Russian. After that Yuschka had shot Tilla a long, leering glance and had dragged the two easy chairs into the corridor, dropped into them, and fallen asleep. The captain closed the door and sat down across from Tilla.

The room was almost dark now as the candles were burning down. It was too dark for Tilla, and too quiet—

quietness underscored, rather than disturbed, by Yuschka's loud snores outside.

"Well, Tilla, Tillatchka," Gorchakov said into the silence, "we are finally alone."

Tilla, her eyes wide, sat frightened and stiff. "Captain, I—"

"Call me Dmitri," he interrupted.

"Deemeetree," she said obediently.

"No! Say it again, Dmitri!"

"Deemeetree."

"No, no, no!" he shouted, and hit his head with both hands. "Not Dee-mee-tree! Dmitri!"

"Mittree."

He laughed. "Try Mitya."

"Mitya."

"Good enough. Mitya it will be." He reached across the table and put his strong, warm hand over hers. It had an immediate effect. She relaxed a little, and when he looked into her eyes, she was able to meet his glance. Never had she seen eyes so truly ultramarine blue.

"Mitya?" she asked timidly. "Why did you get Aunt Liz drunk?"

"Why not?" he replied, and withdrew his hand. He reached for the bottle from which he had poured her drinks. "Have another?"

She held out her glass and watched the white liquid flow into it. "What have you been giving me?"

"What does it taste like?"

"Water."

122

"That's what it is."

"Why?"

He leaned back in his chair, and his scowl turned him from protective Mitya into frightening Russian Captain Gorchakov as he snapped, "Because I don't like my women drunk!" He leaned across the table until his face was only inches away from hers. He gave a short nod toward the couch. "Come on!" he commanded. "Let's go to bed."

"No!"

"I can force you!" he said menacingly. "I can rape you and"—suddenly he held his pistol in his hand—"and I can shoot you." And then, contrary to all expectation, he threw back his head and laughed, put the pistol away and continued laughing, a warm, happy, infectious laugh. Almost hysterical with relief, Tilla joined in. She was still laughing when he slammed his fist on the table and stamped his foot. "This is all wrong!" he said in mock anger. "You are not playing your role right," and he added more seriouly, "Neither am I."

They had gone out on the balcony, stood there in the dark. In the park below, Russian soldiers were gathered around a fire. There was the melancholy sound of a harmonica; one voice joined, then two, three until they were a full chorus, a chorus of deep men's voices that cast a powerful spell. When he gently put his arm around her, she did not move. His breath smelled of alcohol as he whispered urgently into her ear, "Tillatchka! Will you sleep with me?"

Her heart beat as much from the wish to be near him

123

as from fear. When she shook her head, he turned abruptly and went inside. She followed slowly, hesitantly.

He lay down on the couch, arms behind his head. On the wall behind him the shadows of the almost empty bottles looked five feet tall. "Go away!" he said harshly. "Go to your aunt's room. I am a man, Tilla, not a beast! Not like your countrymen, who raped and murdered their way across my country! Blow out the candles and go. Go!" he repeated. "I am tired."

She had carefully climbed over the snoring Yuschka, felt her way into Elizabeth's room, closed the door quietly. Her aunt didn't stir. Tilla stood there in the darkness, then lay down on the rug, curled herself tightly together. She cried, making only the slightest sniffling noise, though she felt like screaming—screaming out her loneliness, her confusion, her horror of the world. So great was her misery that she listened without interest to the frantic banging at the apartment door, heard Yuschka and Mitya talk to each other and Mrs. Scheuermann, the pastor's wife, entreat Mitya to come save her daughters.

She heard a scuffle in the courtyard. Russians shouted; heavy boots ran over gravel. A shot rang out, then another, and a man screamed. It didn't matter to her, but why didn't Mitya come back? Where was he? At last she heard steps. They were his. He talked rapidly to Yuschka, who grunted in response. When the door opened, she feigned sleep. A flashlight searched her out. Mitya spoke in Russian, and then something was thrown over her. The light went out, and the door closed. She wrapped herself in the big coat which smelled of leather, vodka, tobacco, and Mitya, and she finally fell into a troubled sleep.

"Oh, oh, oh!" Elizabeth moaned, holding her head. She sat up and blinked when she saw Tilla sitting on the floor wearing the Russian uniform coat. "Tilla!" she whined. "Oh, Tilla! What could I have done? I shouldn't have left you alone with them, but what could I do?" She waited for her niece to say something. When Tilla didn't, she went on. "He made me drink too much. I was afraid. You never know where you are with these Russians. They are nice one moment and ready to shoot you the next." She paused. "Did they . . . They didn't hurt you . . . did they?"

"No," said Tilla. "Nothing happened."

"Thank God!" Elizabeth sighed. "I thought the captain was a gentleman. He certainly is very handsome, isn't he?"

"Yes," said Tilla. And that was the end of their conversation.

For the three weeks that he remained in the apartment, Captain Gorchakov was cool but polite to Elizabeth, and except on two occasions, he completely ignored Tilla. Once he found her on the staircase talking to Mrs. Feuerlicht. He stamped his foot, turned red with anger, and yelled, "I told you to stay indoors!"

The only other time that he acknowledged her existence was when he saw her moving the cot Paula had given her into the little dressing room. He flew into a fury, yanked the cot out of her hand, and carried it back into Elizabeth's bedroom. "That's where I want you to sleep! And I want you to stay in there when I'm not here!" he shouted as if he were commanding troops. "Don't you understand?" Tilla could only shake her head, and changing his tone, he added softly, "I want you to be safe!"

Captain Gorchakov had saved Tilla and almost everyone else in the house. Day and night he had answered calls for help. When a drunken soldier had threatened old Mr. Muffel because he didn't have a watch, the captain had come to the rescue. He had prevented the looting of Paula's store, the rape of Mrs. Feuerlicht, Mrs. Ahlers, and the Scheuermann daughters (more than once). He had been away when it had happened to Vera Grabetz.

Everyone called him Colonel, and when they spoke of him, he was "our guardian angel," "the perfect gentleman," "the savior," or "*our* Deemeetree."

At the end of May Gorchakov moved. Though a curfew was still in effect, it was possible now even for women to walk in the streets unmolested. Local administrations had been established, and ration cards issued. Slowly order was returning. Dmitri said short and polite farewells and sent Yuschka ahead with his bags, then went once more into the balcony room and called Tilla. When she entered, he immediately closed the door behind her and without warning embraced and kissed her passionately. She returned his embrace and kiss. Then he laughed that happy, boyish laugh and said, "Now you see, you stupid girl, what you have missed?"

From behind her curtain, Mrs. Scheuermann watched the captain's departure. She turned to her husband, the pastor, and said with a sigh, "There he goes. What a wonderful man! What a gentleman . . . and so handsome! I'll never understand what he saw in that little tart!"

23 "Nothing is left in Berlin," wrote the correspondent of the *New York Herald Tribune* on May 3, 1945. "There are no homes, no shops, no transportation, no government buildings. Only a few walls are the heritage bequeathed by the Nazis to the people of Berlin. Berlin can now be regarded only as a geographical location heaped with mountainous mounds of debris."

This description was still accurate three weeks later, despite the fact that lilac and forsythia were in full bloom in Max and Ida's small garden, and the first tulips were about to open.

Rolf worked the old-fashioned pump and followed Ida with the watering can.

"Not that much!" she chided, bending down to straighten her tiny lettuce plants. "How would you like it if I dumped a tubful of cold water on you?"

"Try me!" Rolf challenged her, grinning.

She shook her head. "Too smart for your own good,

that's what you are!" She gave him a friendly shove before she resumed her walk along the row of seedlings, which she mothered like newborn babies. "Now these here! But be careful!" she commanded.

Rolf wasn't listening. He stood idly digging patterns into the sand with the heel of his boot. She stood up and wiped her hands on her apron. "I know what you're thinking, boy! And there's only one way to find out. Go! Maybe Max will come along."

"No. I'll go alone. How long do you think it'll take me?"

She scratched her head. "Two hours, maybe more if it's true that the Spree Bridge was blown up. Yeah, I guess it's all right now as long as you stay away from the Russians. You know they'll grab the first one off the street if one of their prisoners is missing. They don't care who you are as long as they have the right number of heads. Be careful, you hear? And if . . ."

"If you don't find your mother," Rolf completed the sentence for her.

"You can always come back here!" she said. "You know that?" He nodded. "Well then! What are you waiting for? Get going! I'll find you an old tablecloth for your knapsack."

"Why?"

"Why! He asks why! Aside from the fact that Hitler Youth uniforms are not in fashion, I don't want anyone to get cute ideas that you are carrying something useful. I'm going to provision you proper, but not for some *ganef* to come along and take it all away from you, *kapito?* If we knot it all into an old cloth, it will be less conspicuous."

Ten minutes later Rolf was ready and suddenly scared to leave. He felt at home here and was loath to venture out alone into the jungle of ruins.

"Even the longest journey begins with the first step," said Max. "Just put one foot in front of the other, old buddy, and you'll get there." He slapped Rolf on the back. "You'll be all right. This is nothing by comparison to what we've been through, ha?"

"Maybe he should wait a day or two?" Ida cut in, suddenly worried now that he was actually leaving.

"Ah, papperlapapp," said Max. "What's the difference? Today or tomorrow? He's ready now."

"Just be careful!" Ida couldn't help saying it again.

Her husband went on, "And don't accept candy from strangers."

They watched him walk away and waved every time he turned around, as he did often. A slender boy with thin blond hair in worn-out boots, pants that were too short, and Max's jacket, which was far too large, with that odd bundle slung over his shoulder, marched into the distance.

Ida sighed. "That poor boy looks like a scarecrow."

"He's not going to a dance, is he?" Max countered. "It may even help, 'cause who'd want to bother a kid like that?"

Rolf had walked briskly for a time, but the closer he got to the center of town, the more difficult it became. There had been block after block of ruins where, in some places, the rubble lay as high as the third floor. He had traversed these mountains on a kind of footpath. Obviously others had walked there before, but he saw no one. The stench of burned buildings was still strong, and he had been glad to leave this eerie area behind. He met few Germans, and whenever he saw Russians, he had given them wide berth or hidden in ruins.

He was tired and covered with dust. His feet hurt, and his knee was bloody because he had fallen twice, tripped over the flapping sole of his left boot. The Russians had relieved him of his watch, so he didn't know what time it was or how long he had walked, only that it seemed forever. But he had made it. The street sign, amazingly, was still there and clearly read "Bleibtreustrasse." Still there and standing was also the neoclassic entrance to number 36, with its marble columns. Shrapnel-pockmarked entrance to nothing—a pile of rubble that long ago had been his home. There remained of number 36 only the main wall, the staircase from the second to the third floor on one side, and a few square yards of the actual apartments on the other. The staircase, complete with banister, looked oddly glued on. The scene was made even more ridiculous by the fact that the ornate entry doors on the second and third floors were still there as well, properly closed and apparently undamaged. The staircase from second to third, but nothing from the street level to the second. Dumb, totally useless stairs from the second floor to the sky.

He searched the pillars, the remaining wall, even large pieces of concrete for messages like the ones he had seen on many other ruins: "Bergmann & Guensche all alive now Gatow Waldstrasse 7." There were none. "How the hell does she expect me to find her?" he said aloud angrily, then kicked a stone with all the frustration in his heart. Shit! Now he had stubbed his toe—on top of everything else.

He had thought to ask at the grocery story, but it was no longer there. A burned-out antiaircraft gun stood in the pile of rubble where it had been. "Shit! Shit! Shit!" he mumbled to himself, not knowing what to do next. Then he saw an old man, pail in hand, turn the corner.

"Excuse me, sir," he said politely. "Would you by any chance know the whereabouts of anyone from number thirty-six?"

The old man eyed him wearily. "They're either in heaven or hell—depending," he said, and was about to move on, but Rolf held him by his sleeve.

"Are you sure?"

"Sure as I'm standing here," the old man growled. "They made me dig for them after that big raid. But we were too late—suffocated, all of 'em. They were *dead*. Take my word for it."

Rolf stared up at the part of the house that still stood, at the two parts of apartments that had survived it all. Whatever was still up there was so covered with debris as to be unidentifiable. He thought that the top apartment was his mother's, had been his home, but he couldn't be sure. Yet it must be. He tried to picture it, as it had been. Edith's neat study and his own room, with his father's big black leather chair and, and, and . . . Rolf sat down and couldn't even cry.

Looking neither left nor right, he listlessly started back on the long road to Max and Ida. He would have to hurry in order to be back before curfew, but he dragged his feet. He didn't care about the curfew, didn't care about anything as he slogged past the long line of people waiting their turn at the pump. When he had gone two or three blocks, the thought struck him that those things, whatever they were, remaining on the third floor were rightfully his and that he somehow had to get whatever was still usable. Build a mountain, find a crane, borrow a ladder—there must be a way to get up there. He decided to go back for another look, the better to be able to describe the situation to Max. Max would know what to do.

He walked fast now, almost ran. As he approached the ruin of his home for the second time, he thought of something else. How could she have written him, "We are bombed out," if she had died in that cellar? It wasn't logical. She had been somewhere else when it happened. Rolf, for the first time, allowed himself the smallest bit of hope.

Once more he stood in front of Bleibtreustrasse 36, staring up at the inaccessible staircase and the closed door on top. Weird, incongruous sight. He could even see the bronze nameplate. He couldn't read it, but he knew the inscription, Dr. H. Severin. And then, as he looked at it, the door opened.

Rolf couldn't believe his eyes. He was certain that he was either mad or seeing things. It couldn't be. But it was. A rope ladder in one hand and an ordinary pail in the other, his mother was coming down that staircase.

The whole scene was unreal. A gigantic stage set. The afternoon sun a huge klieg light, spotlighting the diva, who slowly descended from that staircase in the sky.

He wanted to rush up, jump up to her, and scream with joy, but no sound would come.

Edith, who had seen him, clung to the shaky banister and then sat down. She, too, wanted to shout, "Rolf, my son!" but her mouth and throat were full of dust and "Rolf" became nothing more than a hoarse whisper. She was shaking so badly that she dropped the rope ladder. It took Rolf many tries to get it back up to her, and then she was too excited to catch it. When she had finally caught and attached it, they promptly both climbed on. As she was climbing down, he was climbing up. When he realized his mistake, he jumped off and caught his mother in his open arms.

24 After Dmitri left, Tilla had moved her cot into the tiny dressing room, which was now hers. The old wooden wardrobe took up most of the space in it, dresser and cot the rest. Yet Tilla had managed to get the bike in as well. That's why Elizabeth called it the storage room, but Tilla, considering it her most important piece of furniture, refused to put it back in the cellar.

When she finally thought about it, she had had small hope of ever seeing it again. But Paula remembered that in the rush of that day she had put it in the first handy place, behind the open cellar door. When Tilla rushed downstairs, she had found it there; even the bag was still on the handlebar. Triumphantly she had presented her aunt with eleven old potatoes and three onions. They had shoots the length of an arm; but Elizabeth had turned them into potato pancakes that very night, and they invited Paula and Vera Grabetz to celebrate with them.

She idly kicked the pedals with the heels of her boots. With the stand flipped down, she could pedal it, pretend that she was riding through lush valleys or mysterious woods. She leaned on the board which she had tied over the handlebars. It was desk, drawing board, and dream place, all rolled into one.

In the center of the wall, right over her cot, hung Mr. Troester's old canvas bag. She looked at it and thought of Lotte Palitz, the girl who had dragged her off the street, who was now her friend. She thought about all the things Lotte had told her, how hard the Nazi years had been for the Palitzes because they were communists and how the Nazis had killed Lotte's sister in a concentration camp. *But Lotte still has her parents*, she thought with envy, *and now she has Folker, too.* The doorbell rang, and hearing Lotte's voice, she went to greet her.

Lotte's cheeks were redder than usual, and her long brown ponytail swung wildly. It was long enough to reach her rear end, if she ever stood still.

"Come along!" Lotte urged, taking Tilla by the hand, "I have to show you what Folker and I have found."

"Just a minute," Elizabeth objected, coming out of the kitchen. "Where are you going?"

"Do you know Nazi Neuberger's estate on Waldstrasse?" was Lotte's answer. "It's the one with the big stone wall and iron gate."

"I know it," said Elizabeth.

"You must promise not to tell anyone, Mrs. Hoffart. We found a cherry tree there."

"What were you doing in their garden?" Elizabeth asked sharply.

"*Their* garden?" Lotte sneered. "It all belonged to the Loewenthals—until the Nazis came. The Neubergers moved in after the Loewenthals conveniently 'disappeared.' Neuberger, an unskilled laborer, suddenly became the owner of an estate. You didn't know that?" When Elizabeth said nothing, Lotte went on. "Anyway, they committed suicide. There's no one there now, so why shouldn't we pick the cherries?" She tugged at Tilla's arm. "If we don't hurry, someone else may find them."

"Be careful!" Elizabeth said, shaking her head in disapproval. "And be back before dark."

"Tilla," Lotte said once they were on the street, "I want to ask you something." She chewed on the end of her ponytail, then blurted out, "Does it hurt?"

Tilla stopped and looked at her. "What are you talking about?"

"Oh, you know what I mean?" Lotte said, blushing. "We are friends, aren't we? I promise you I won't tell anyone . . . I just want to know!"

"Know what?" Tilla asked. Then, as she realized what Lotte meant, the blood rushed to her face. "Now you, too! I have to disappoint you. I can't tell you anything because I did not sleep with Captain Gorchakov. That's what you mean, isn't it?"

Lotte nodded and said, with surprise in her voice, "You didn't?"

"NO, I DID NOT!" Tilla almost screamed. "I know that everyone thinks I did, even *you,* but I didn't."

"Don't get sore," Lotte said, trying to pacify her. "I wouldn't blame you if you had. He was so nice and so very handsome—"

"I told you I didn't!"

"I believe you," Lotte said with a disappointed sigh. "It's just that I'm dying to know how it is. . . . Have you ever done it?"

136

"No."

"Aren't you curious?"

"Yes . . . and scared."

"Me, too. But maybe they all make too much of it."

"I don't know. Maybe it's better than . . ."

"I have a hunch that I'll soon find out. I almost did . . ."

"With Folker?"

"*Hm.*" But now that Tilla was interested, Lotte changed the subject. "I can't wait for you to see that garden and the mansion. It must have been absolutely gorgeous before everything was broken and smashed. Still, the bathrooms are intact, and they are something you see only in movies."

"I don't want to go into that house."

"Oh, yes, you do. One is as large as your aunt's living room. It's all marble, even the big sunken tub, and the windows reach all the way down to the floor, so that you can see the garden when you're taking a bath. All the rooms have parquet floors, and there are big double sliding glass doors between the rooms. The glass is all broken, but you can still see what a fantastic place it must have been. You'll never see one like it again!"

"I'll own one someday," Tilla said as if she were stating an obvious fact.

Lotte looked at her and laughed. "Such modest goals! Invite me sometime when you've got it!" she joked.

"I will."

The garden was almost a park and magnificent indeed, even in its unattended, overgrown state. There were stately oaks, elms, and lindens. White birches contrasted with the dark green foliage of spruce and pines. Philodendron and mountain laurel, spiraea bushes and peonies all bloomed in profusion. Roses added their splendor and aroma. This fairy-tale garden was basking in the July sun, and the villa with its broken windows made it almost magical.

"And now for our lunch," Lotte said, proudly pointing to the birch grove. "That's where our tree is hiding."

"Lunch?"

"The cherries! That is, if no one else has found them."

They climbed up to perch in the middle of the tree like two bright birds, picking, chewing, and bombarding each other with the pits. Lotte saw him coming but had her mouth full of cherries, and by the time she had swallowed them he had put a finger over his lips, then uttered a resounding "BOO!"

"Rolf!" Tilla cried. "Rolf!" And then said his name once more: "Rolf."

"How did you know we were here?" Lotte asked.

"From Elizabeth, of course. I went to the house first."

Between bites of cherries and alternately flipping his pits at Lotte and Tilla, he related his adventures. When he came to the part where Ida wailed, "Oh, my poor baby," the girls laughed so hard that the whole tree shook. "But I really did get sick!" Rolf complained, making them laugh even more.

"I told you he's got a weak stomach!" Tilla giggled.

"I'd say," agreed Lotte, "if one bottle of vodka is enough to make him sick. Tilla drinks vodka like water!"

Tilla shot Lotte a withering look just as a pit from Rolf hit her squarely on the forehead.

Lotte made a fist, threatened Rolf. But he was out of her reach. "Don't worry," she said. "I'll get even! Shall we look at the house now?"

Rolf gallantly helped them climb down, and as Tilla descended, his hands spanned her waist, then slid up to her breasts, feeling them for just an instant. He smiled and, hanging cherries over her ear, nodded approval.

They walked, single file, through the tall grass, and as they passed the roses, Rolf tore off a red one, which he handed Tilla with a bow, and a pink one, which he gave to Lotte.

"Don't think that this will get you off the hook!" Lotte said, sniffing it before putting it between her teeth.

When they reached the flagstone terrace with the two big stone lions, Rolf climbed on the nearer one. Assuming the stance of the Fuehrer, he bellowed: "And we shall erase their cities!" He jumped off, turned, and now saluted the imaginary Fuehrer, shouting, "HEIL! HEIL! HEIL!"

"I've had enough of that shit, Hitler boy!" Lotte said angrily as she dropped the rose. She purposely stepped on it and walked into the house.

Rolf shrugged his shoulders, took Tilla into his arms, and kissed her. Kissed her firmly on the mouth and tried to part her lips with his tongue. "Angel!" he said releasing her. "I'll have to teach you how to kiss." And with a playful slap on her behind he ran into the house, screaming, "Lotte! Lotte!"

139

"What?" came the answer from above.

"Do you know how to kiss?" he yelled, and when there was no answer, he bounded up the stairs.

Tilla followed slowly. When she reached the upper floor, she saw them on the balcony. Rolf was holding Lotte by her ponytail, bending her backward over the railing and trying to kiss her. Tilla stood in the dusty room, among the pieces of smashed furniture and broken glass, and thought of Mitya and Rolf . . . and then the balcony was empty. It ran the full length of the house and they had obviously left through another room. Tilla stepped out onto the balcony now, stood where they had stood.

The air was heavy; not a single leaf moved. Cicadas shrilled. Tilla listened to the footsteps inside the house until Lotte, followed by Rolf, raced up to her, touched her, gasping, "You're it!" before she was gone again. After that they chased each other through the rubble and debris of the ransacked villa until they were out of breath. Each leaned in a different doorway of the large downstairs room leading to the terrace. Rolf, still panting, made a sweeping gesture over it. "This," he declared, "will be my music room! My Bechstein will go—"

"Was your father a Nazi?" Lotte interrupted him. "Is he still alive?"

"My father died in 1936," Rolf said, lighting a cigarette. Puffing out a big cloud, he added, "In Dachau, if that means anything to you."

Lotte, clearly taken aback, said, "Dachau! Does that

mean anything to me? Does Ravensbrueck mean anything to you?"

"Your father?"

"My sister."

"So?" said Rolf.

"So?" Lotte screamed. "So? So! What do you mean, so? Why did your father die in Dachau? And if he did, how come you were in the Hitler Youth and still scream '*Heil*'?"

Rolf looked at her with an amused smile. "You want my life history in one sentence? I did the *Heil* bit for fun. Can't you take a joke?"

"It's not funny to me!" Lotte said.

Rolf took another drag from his cigarette. "Here," he offered. "Want to try?"

"No, thank you!"

"Would you rather kiss?" he asked, smirking.

"Can't you ever be serious?"

"I've been serious far too long. That's my problem. I can't begin to tell you how seriously afraid I've been." He shook a finger at Lotte and said in mock earnestness, "Being scared shitless is a very serious matter. When you fall backward into your own foxhole from the backfire of your own rifle, *that* is damn serious, you'll have to agree. Just thinking about it can make you frown for a month. Anyway, what do you want me to do, cry? That won't bring back my father, or your sister and all the others. Will it?"

"So you crack jokes and say, 'Forget it.' Don't you see

141

that we'll have to be the ones who make sure that it never happens again? We'll have to stick together. God knows there are very few of us; the Nazis saw to that. Let me tell you something! All Germans who were not actively against Hitler must be held responsible for the concentration camps and the destruction—"

"But everyone has suffered," Tilla interrupted meekly. "I lost my whole family."

"But that's different!" said Lotte in a tone of superiority. "Your people were for Hitler—"

"They weren't really. I mean—"

"Tilla!" Lotte sounded exasperated. "If they weren't for him, they didn't do anything to prevent him either, did they? So in effect they got what they deserved, I'm sorry to say . . . and," she added quickly, "sorry for you, of course."

"What did *you* do to prevent Hitler?" Rolf asked, blowing a big cloud of smoke her way. He went on before she could answer. "For such a little girl, you have a pretty big mouth!"

"Get lost!"

"Get lost!" said a man's voice behind them, almost as an echo. "What are you doing here anyway?" He was a small man in a shabby business suit and now stepped aside to allow three others into the room. The others were tall foreign men and wore natty officers' uniforms. They talked with the German in a foreign tongue—and it wasn't Russian.

Rolf, Tilla, and Lotte stared at them and the unfamiliar

uniforms until the German admonished, "Didn't you hear what I said? Scram, kids! This is going to be quarters for the French general. Beat it!"

At that moment Rolf jumped up and shouted, *"Vive la France! Vive la France!"*

"Vive la Soviet Union," mumbled Lotte as they left.

Rolf was jubilant as they walked to the station. He repeated over and over again, "They're here at last. The Western Allies are finally here—and it's about time. And it inspires me. Oh, what inspiration!" he shouted as he got between Tilla and Lotte. He put his arms around them and recited:

> His heart beat wildly
> He got quite warm
> As he held the young lovelies
> One in each arm.

People stared because he spoke so loudly, then smiled. As he boarded the train, Rolf handed Tilla a flat little package, kissed them both, and was gone.

"He's a strange one," Lotte remarked. "I don't mean it in a bad sense—and—I'm sorry for what I said earlier," she added. "I didn't mean to hurt you. You know that, don't you? We are still friends, yes?"

"Yes," Tilla said. "We're still friends."

The package had contained a book. Jack London's *The Call of the Wild* and there was a handwritten dedication:

"For Tillangel with those big gray eyes, to remind
her of
  R ufus
  O ld truck
  L olling in hay
  F alling in love

That day one of the entries in the ledger of the city of
Berlin read:

Berlin, July 4, 1945.
  Today U.S. and British forces, together with
the French detachment, entered their several
sectors of Berlin—in accordance with the agreement reached at the conference of Commanders
in Chief of the three Armies of Occupation. . . .

. . . . . .

25 "NO! NO! NO!" Professor Seewald shouted in
a feeble old man's voice. He wrung his hands
in frustration, clapped them over his ears,
then gestured and looked at the ceiling as if beseeching a
higher authority. "You're pounding, but it is not a drum!
This is a very fine instrument!" His thumbs rubbed over
the tips of his fingers. "It's sensitive, subtle. You had that
sensitivity. Where has it gone?" The professor sadly shook
his head. "I know, I know, the war has brutalized us all.

But you can't be brutal and make good music. It is mutually exclusive."

Rolf looked at his hands on the yellowed keys of the formidable Steinway grand, then watched Seewald walk back and forth on the threadbare carpet. The professor looked like nothing so much as a scarecrow in his once-elegant but now-shabby dark suit. It wasn't the suit that seemed too large; it appeared rather that the professor had shriveled and shrunk inside it. "Shall I try again?" Rolf asked.

Seewald nodded, then sang, "Da-dah-dahdah-da-daah, andante, pianissimo," as he tapped out the rhythm with his foot. He did not interrupt this time but waited until the last note faded away. "Better, my boy. At least it wasn't offensive. Let's leave it at that for today, shall we?"

Rolf got up, gathered the sheet music, and closed the piano. "See you later," he said as he went to the door.

"Where are you going?"

"Don't know yet."

"You'll be back for dinner?"

Rolf turned. "What dinner? I didn't know we had anything in the house!"

The old professor helplessly shrugged his shoulders. "Habit of speech, I suppose. Sorry. You're right. There isn't anything. Maybe your mother . . ." He was left to listen to the door being shut.

Edith Severin sighed as she walked upstairs. It was all very depressing. She had mistakenly assumed that every-

145

thing would be easier, better once the war was over, and now it was almost as if the very opposite had happened. She had to remind herself how lucky she was to have Rolf back, lucky, too, to have met her father's old friend Professor Seewald and that he had invited them to share his spacious but stuffy apartment, which had somehow survived the war almost undamaged. Where would they have found a place to live in this city of rubble? Where could she have found a piano for Rolf, much less a Steinway grand? Yes, she had reason to thank her lucky stars also for the fact that Seewald was home to keep an eye on Rolf while she was at work at the newspaper. And on top of that he gave Rolf lessons, charging her only a minimum fee. She had no doubt that Rolf would become a fine pianist. Seewald thought so, too. He should know, having been internationally renowned himself. Audiences had showered him with flowers at every concert he gave. Couldn't have found a better teacher if she'd tried. The music, she reflected, was the only thing Rolf took seriously, the only area where he showed the old man any respect. Maybe she worried too much, she told herself, worried about Rolf, about the old man. Worried that they would not have enough food. Worried about the winter ahead. All newspapers had had to print the notice of the Allied *Kommandatura*, that there would not be any coal or wood for heating purposes for the civilian population. Because it was summer, no one wanted to believe it. But wait until it got cold. Seewald was so frail, and Rolf nothing but skin and bones at an age where he should have had plenty of food. She didn't know what they'd do. She sighed as she opened the apartment door and entered the kitchen.

"Edith!" A startled Professor Seewald exclaimed as he nervously hid something behind his back. His wrinkled old face, under the white hair, slowly turned red as he looked at Edith with an expression of terror.

"What are you doing?" Edith asked, walking toward him. With a helpless gesture he stepped aside, giving Edith a full view of the beautiful small letter scale of polished brass. On the left pan lay three sparkling weights: 100 grams, 50 grams, and the smallest, 25 grams. On the other pan, perfectly balancing the combined 175 grams, lay one piece of bread. *The* bread. All the bread they had.

"I-I," the professor stammered.

Edith wearily sat down on a kitchen chair. "You think that you're not getting your fair share, is that it?" she asked without looking at him. And when he didn't reply, she said harshly, "Answer me, Seewald! Why don't you come out and say it?"

"I just wanted to find out," he said meekly.

"You just wanted to find out how many grams we cheat you. Is that it? We all get the same ration. Twenty-two grams of bread a day. It's known as the starvation or cemetery ration, Seewald! I've been cutting that bread as evenly as I know how. But if you want to weigh every crumb on your scale, go ahead. I won't stop you. Next time we get bread, weigh your damned, lousy twenty-two grams and take it and lock it up in your room. Go ahead, lock it up!"

The professor sank, dwindled into a sitting position on

the other chair without making a sound. "I'm so hungry, Edith. I'm sorry, but I'm so hungry. It seems I'm always hungry," he wailed, and then covered his face with his hands.

"Aren't we all?" she said softly. "But I don't know what to do." She leaned forward and rested her elbows on her knees. "What's becoming of us, Seewald? How can we live like this?" There were only muted sobs for an answer. She slowly got up and walked over to him, gently put her arm around his shoulders. "There'll be dinner tonight, Seewald. A friend at the office gave me a cabbage and a few potatoes."

"You have it. You and the boy eat it," he said, still hiding his face. Then he suddenly took his hands away and looked at her. "I don't have any more coupons," he said as big tears rolled down the furrows of his cheeks.

"Oh, for heaven's sake!" Edith said as she let go of his shoulders. "Pull yourself together. I know that you don't have any coupons, and neither do we. I told you, I got the cabbage from a friend. She didn't ask me for coupons. It's from her garden. You'll eat with us. As always, we'll share, you know that! By the way, where is Rolf?"

"I don't know," Seewald replied as he dried his eyes. "He went out."

"Did he say where he was going?"

"No."

"He didn't go to school, did he?"

"No . . . but he practiced for three hours, Edith!"

"You don't have to cover up for him. I'm grateful, Seewald, that you teach him. I don't expect you to baby-sit. He's too old for that anyway. I know he doesn't listen, and aside from his music, I don't know what he's up to."

"He's gifted, Edith, and he does work hard; but I don't know, somehow his heart doesn't seem to be in it."

"Maybe he's distracted by the rumblings of his empty stomach?" She looked at him, but he averted his eyes. "Do you think it's that girl?"

"Could be. I don't know. He doesn't tell me anything."

"That's the problem," she agreed. "He doesn't tell me anything either." They both looked at the door. "Well," said Edith, "speak of the devil."

"Hello, Edith," Rolf said, beaming at his mother and kissing her. "Hey, Seewald."

"We were just talking about you."

Rolf stopped smiling. "So I gather. Talking about why I don't go to school, like a good little boy, no doubt." His voice skipped an octave as he screamed, "Why should I waste my time listening to those old Nazi assholes?"

"Rolf!" Edith reprimanded him sharply. "Mind your language! Curse words are not a substitute for an intelligent argument!"

"*You* can argue in-tel-li-gent-ly until you're blue in the face!" Rolf interrupted her. "But an asshole will remain an asshole!"

"You think you're smart, don't you?" Edith said angrily. "You know everything already. You don't have to go to school, oh, no. Your Latin and French are as perfect as your punctuation and grammar . . . and don't tell me

149

about Nazis! If your teachers were Nazis, they wouldn't be allowed to teach!"

"Oh, no, wouldn't they? Well, Editor Severin, I have news for *you!* Remember a certain Dr. Berthold Betz? He was the guy you entrusted your precious little boy to when they took him to camp, if I may refresh your memory . . . and that selfsame Dr. Betz fled when the Russians came, leaving your little boy all alone. He was a Nazi if I ever saw one. But my dear, smart mother, he can teach, because he managed never to become an official, card-carrying member of the Nazi Party. He was a Nazi, and he still is a Nazi, *and* he is teaching your son. Isn't that nice? And *you* expect me to listen to *that* guy? To sit there and . . . ah! Anyway, here I come home with good news, and what do I get? Another lecture!"

"What good news?"

"Would you like to know?" he asked teasingly, a grin spreading over his face, as he quickly ducked an affectionate punch from his mother. "I got a job! That's the good news. A job where I will get double rations!" he said proudly. "I signed up to clear rubble."

His announcement was greeted with stunned silence. It was the professor who first found words. "Are you out of your mind?" he cried as he took Rolf by his shoulders and shook him. "Clear rubble with *your* hands?"

"That's the way it's done!" Rolf impertinently interrupted.

"But you'll ruin your hands! If you do that, you can forget about becoming a pianist!"

"I can also forget about becoming a pianist, or anything else for that matter, if I starve to death," Rolf replied angrily as he walked out and slammed the door behind him.

26

"Tilla! You slammed the door!" Elizabeth called accusingly after her. "Look, you don't *have* to go!"

"I'm going! And I'm sorry about the door," Tilla replied as she bounded down the stairs.

"Clump, clump, clump," said Elizabeth to herself, closing the door. *She looks like a sylph but walks like an elephant.* She stood and listened to the fading sound of Tilla's steps. October 26. *In three days Tilla is going to be sixteen. And for her to have a birthday cake I have to send her to the black market. It's really horrible. Maybe I shouldn't have let her go? Well, she's been there before.* She tried to allay her fears.

Elizabeth sighed and thought of that last packet of cigarettes, which Tilla carried in her pocket, to barter for butter and sugar. She also thought of Major Macdonnell, her boss, charming and shrewd. "You left your cigarettes, Mrs. Hoffart," he had told her, pointing to the ones *he* had left by her typewriter. Others might have seized the opportunity and grabbed them then and there, but she had coolly replied, "They are yours, not mine." It had made a favorable impression on him. Not only had he given her the cigarettes, but he had also insisted he would try to help her in other ways. *Too bad the English ones are so perfumy*, she thought. *I guess I'll have to get used to them.* The major occupied her mind in many ways. Last but not least was the question of whether he'd get her some butter or meat. *Maybe I won't have to send her there anymore. I hope this is the last time.*

This was the first time that Tilla was going to the black market alone, without Lotte and Folker. She was not so self-assured as she had led her aunt to believe. Maybe she wouldn't have to go there anymore, now that her aunt worked for the British Military Government of Berlin. Luckily she had found a generous boss. Tilla heard her aunt's voice in her head, saying, "Luck had nothing to do with it! I got that job because of my English. I told you how important it is to study foreign languages!" And Tilla immediately began to dread tonight's vocabulary session.

A cold autumn wind blew leaves and bits of paper off the platform onto the tracks as Tilla stepped out of the train. She instantly spotted the small cracked mirror on the rusty candy machine. Elbowing people aside, she went to it, just to see herself once more, to admire her new short permanent wave, her red-lipsticked mouth and again to smile at the one it reflected. Then, digging her hands deep into the pockets of her camel's hair coat, she resolutely walked into the crowd.

There were, as usual, the Russian soldiers buying watches,

152

clocks, anything that ticked or moved. There were the Americans looking for cameras, binoculars, silver, porcelain, and Hummel figurines—paying with their PX rations and American cigarettes, or Amis, as everyone called them. Money, the old shabby reichsmark, had no value. The real currency was Amis.

She shook her head at the white-haired woman who mumbled, "It's real silver, miss. Six Amis or a bread," while allowing her a quick glimpse at an ornate bowl. Tilla turned her back on those shady characters, men with shifty eyes and foreign accents, who offered everything from real coffee to nylons and fur coats "for a little loving." They scared her even with Lotte and Folker at her side. One in particular had the habit of sidling up the minute they arrived. And sure enough, there he was, putting his hairy, flabby, bejeweled hand on her arm. She pointedly ignored him, and with an insinuating smile he melted back into the crowd. But she had the uncomfortable feeling that his eyes followed her. If only she could tell a policeman; but this was the black market, and if police appeared, she'd have to run as fast as everyone else.

There was the old man with the kindly face. She'd seen him before, too. He was holding, in shaky hands, two black straw hats decorated with large, gaily colored silk flowers. They probably had belonged to his wife. No one seemed interested in his hats or his feeble pleas to buy them for something, anything to eat. Feeling sorry for him, she hurried by in search of the butterwoman, a fat peasant who had promised her a pound of butter and a pound of sugar

153

in exchange for Amis—an unspecified amount of Amis. Tilla hoped that she wouldn't ask for more than one pack. Her eyes searched the crowd, those peddling their belongings, willing to sell the shirts off their backs for anything edible, and the others, the profiteers with greedy eyes. The butterwoman wasn't there. She was beginning to get nervous when after her second round she still hadn't found her. This was no place to linger. More than one person was said to have disappeared from here and was later found dead in the ruins. The possibility of a raid did nothing to ease her mind.

To separate herself from the wheeling, dealing black-market crowd and to get a better overall view, she went across the street. Sure enough. There, parked among other vehicles, was Max's banged-up green truck. She had seen it every time she'd been here, but never Max. She was glad of that. This was a place where no one wanted to be seen. But she couldn't help wondering in which of the surrounding ruins he conducted his deals. The truck beckoned, drew her like a magnet. She tried the door on the passenger side and found it open and then couldn't resist the temptation to get in. She sat where she had sat with Rolf, saw the same old jumble of things, and inhaled the familiar vile odor.

Suddenly people were running past, screaming, "RAZZIA! RAZZIA!" She slid off the seat, huddled on the floor, and, desperate to be invisible, pulled the coat over her head.

Police whistles shrilled. There was a staccato sound of high heels, followed by faster clomps of heavy shoes. The

154

truck shook as someone fell against it. A man's authoritative voice said, "You again!"

"Don't know what you mean!" a woman shrieked so close Tilla could hear her inhale. "I ain't never been here before! I ain't done nothing! You can't arrest me!"

"Want to bet?" said the man, obviously a policeman.

"Let go! Don't you dare touch me!" the woman screamed. Tilla heard the door handle rattle. She stopped breathing. There was a scuffle outside.

"Come on, Marge. Don't give me any trouble, you old—" The policeman cursed, and the woman retaliated by calling him a bastard, then worse. But they were going away and had not seen her. Tilla listened until she could no longer make out the obscenities they exchanged. But she didn't dare move. In the distance she still heard the commands of officers and the angry voices of those now being herded into the police vans. Engines started one after the other and rumbled away. It was quiet, but not for long.

Almost immediately there were tentative footsteps, shuffling feet, the murmur of voices becoming louder, bolder. "Ludicrous! Simply ludicrous!" a woman said with righteous indignation. "They should round up the professional black marketeers and those, those whores, of course. That's what the police are for! But I will never understand why decent citizens, like us, shouldn't be allowed to buy food. After all, it's our own silver and jewelry! It's bad enough that I have to sell the ring Albert gave me . . ."

Tilla didn't wait to hear more. She quickly sneaked out of the truck, mingled with the mass of people returning to

155

the square. Bartering and bargaining were in full swing again. The place looked as it had half an hour earlier, as if there never had been a razzia. But the butterwoman was not there. Tilla gave up and decided to head for home. To hell with the cake.

Max, about to climb into his truck, saw her. He watched her cross the street and disappear into the station. "That was . . ." he said aloud. "I'm sure it was. Well, I'll be darned!"

27 The icy north wind rattled windows and doors, and howling seemed to reach right into the stovepipe, pulling out every bit of warmth. Tilla held her cold hands close over Yuschka, as they had named the iron stove. She was grateful that Mitya hadn't taken it along, and Paula had insisted that they keep it. Two days to Christmas. If only it would snow; that at least would make everything look less dismal and depressing. She stretched and counted her work. *Ten folders at five marks each, that's fifty. Thirty bookmarks at one-fifty is forty-five.* The doorbell interrupted her, and she went to open the door. Outside stood a shivering Rolf.

"Tilla, my angel!"

"Hello, Rolf."

"Is that all I get? 'Hello, Rolf,'" he said, imitating her toneless voice.

"Five months is a long time."

"You live too far, angel. Do you know that it took me almost two hours to get here?"

"You got up early."

"Never went to bed! Can't go to bed when you plan a journey like this. Honestly, it's too damn far."

"You might have written. In case you don't know it, mail is being delivered again—ever since July!"

"Did you really think I'd forgotten you?" She shrugged her shoulders. "I'll never forget you," he said earnestly. "How can I? Especially now that you have turned into—"

"What?"

"Let me in and I'll tell you."

"What do you know? Tilla has a studio!" he exclaimed when she led him into her room. "Did you do all this?" he asked, obviously impressed as he looked at the water-colors, which covered most of the floor and every available surface. "They're beautiful! What do you do with them?"

"Sell them to make money for art school," she explained, while quickly gathering up her work. "This is a folder for stationery; those are bookmarks. Over there are the postcards, which go with the sets. I have better things, but when you do so many . . . It seems I can't make enough. Paula's old stock is all but gone, and she can't get anything new because her wholesaler was bombed out.

There isn't anything for people to buy."

"Tilla the artist! You really are an artist. I like it," Rolf said. He climbed on the bike and rang the bell.

"Careful! Don't get the water over anything. Let me clear the cot; that's a better place for you to sit."

He obediently sat down on the cot, watching her as she moved neat piles, listening to her rapid, nervous talk.

"I'll tell you how it started. Paula has been so nice to me. She gave me the cot and a lot of clothes. I wanted to thank her but couldn't think of anything until I thought of designing stationery for her. Then I ended up by making a folder to put it in and matching postcards and book-marks. A whole set with a floral design similar to this one. She was so pleased that she displayed it in her store. When everyone wanted to buy it, she asked me if I could do more. I still have over a hundred orders. My aunt—"

"Is she home?"

"No. She left for work just before you came."

"Hurrah! We are alone!" Rolf rejoiced. "And I have all day!"

"Let me make some tea and put more wood on. You must be—"

"Did you hear what I said?"

"You're cold, let me—"

"Why don't you warm me?"

"The tea will warm you."

"I don't want any tea. I want *you!* Please come here, Tilla." Rolf leaned forward, reached for her, but she ducked behind the bike.

"How do you like my desk?"

"Very clever—but why don't you come here?"

"Do you know that Lotte—"

"I don't want to hear about Lotte! I want to hear about you."

"I'm trying to tell you."

"You can tell me better if you sit next to me."

"I can tell you from where I am."

Rolf leaned back and hit his head on the canvas bag, making her laugh. He pushed it aside, looked at her, brown eyes holding gray ones. "Please come here, Tilla. I want to kiss you. Remember I promised to teach you how to kiss, or have you learned in the meantime?" When she didn't answer, he looked suddenly sad, a pale, vulnerable boy who asked quietly, "Don't you love me anymore? Is there someone else?"

She shook her head and slowly came around the bike. "I still love you. I thought about you all the time. It's just . . ." He pulled her into his lap, held her tightly, kissed her until she kissed him back.

"That wasn't bad—for beginners." He smiled at her. "Tilla, you are beautiful."

"No, I'm not!" She got up before he had a chance to hold her back. "My nose is much too long, and my chin sticks out, and my hair—"

"And sometimes you are silly," he said, and, seeing that she was feeding the fire, added, "Don't waste that wood. Come on, let's get under the cover to get warm."

She watched him take off his jacket and shoes, didn't

159

stop him when he slid under the blanket, only said coolly, "I hope you're comfortable."

"Very," he answered, smiling from ear to ear. "Come and join me."

"I don't lie in bed in the morning!"

"Why not? I do it all the time. Try it."

"I've got work to do," she snapped, getting on her bike. She picked up a brush and dipped it into the water jar. "You suddenly appear after five long months, and all you can think of is how to get me into bed."

"You believe that, Tilla?" She didn't answer and didn't look at him but rubbed the brush so angrily over the Prussian blue that it spattered. "You really think that I have to travel two hours," Rolf went on, "to go to bed with a woman? No, angel. I can have more women than I'd know what to do with."

"I bet."

"Tilla! You can sneer, but it's the truth. My line of work attracts them."

"You work?"

"Tickle the ivories, bar musician, jazz pianist. I do stints here and there. I haven't slept at all, worked all night— didn't go to bed, came straight from work to you."

"Then you must be tired."

"One gets used to it. Now, will you please come here so that I can at least look at you without wrenching my neck? I won't do anything you don't want me to do."

She went to him, sat down hesitantly. Perched on the edge of the cot, she looked straight ahead. When his hand reached for hers, she allowed him to take it. Holding hands, they talked and talked about how they met, relived every detail of their trip.

When she shivered, he lifted a corner of the blanket, made room for her. It seemed natural to get in. Snuggled up against each other, they told their secrets, whispered their hopes for the future, as if too loud a word would rip the fragile threads, tear down the dreams of Steinway on parquet floor, easel under skylight. . . . They held each other, as if their combined warmth could hatch these images and make them real.

When Rolf got up and undressed, she went to the window, pulled drape over drape. The stove made small crackling, hissing noises as she took off her clothes. He put his arm around her waist, walked her over to the old wardrobe. She looked once, then quickly closed her eyes, as they stood naked in front of the dull mirror. Slender boy and girl of the same height, the same hair, the same bony, long-fingered hands.

They went to bed then. His breath was hot and moist in her ear when he explained that he would be cautious, that one would fit into the other, that it was meant that way. And after a first shock of short-lived pain it had felt that way.

"You want to know how you look?" he asked her afterward as he traced the bridge of her nose with his finger. "You look a little smug. Just a little, and very much like the girl in a painting we had at home. You have the same haughty nostrils and determined forehead. The chin, too, but especially your eyes. They are the same as hers, cool and warm at the same time. I've got to find a reproduction of that painting. You reminded me of it when I met you. Vaguely then, but now you look exactly like her. I knew even as a little boy that my wife would look like that."

"We are not married."

"But we will be. We'll get married when I give my first concert, right afterward, that very evening. Seewald says it will take me four to five years, but he's getting senile. Greiner at the conservatory thinks I could be ready in a year. That is, if I devote myself solely to my art and stop prostituting my talent in dives, as he puts it. But if I didn't do that, there'd be no money for tuition and no food at home, facts the good Greiner prefers to ignore. Goetz, at least, has the good sense to let me sleep through his musical theory courses. I'll have to make it up eventually, I know. Anyway, the conservatory sure beats the old high school and all those Nazi assholes."

"Don't mention Nazis and school. I can't wait to get out of that place. Remember that Lotte said most of the teachers and students were Nazis? She was right."

"How's the big mouth?"

"Big mouth is right. That's what got us into a mess. And then she conveniently moved to East Berlin. Her father's been made deputy mayor of Prenzlauer Berg district."

"Tell me about the mess!"

"It's a long story. You really want to hear it?"

"Yes, I want to hear it. Of course, I want to hear every-

162

thing that concerns you, and we have plenty of time."

"It began in geography, when Dr. Paul talked about beautiful Nuremberg. 'A city,' she said, 'noted for its toys and *Lebkuchen*.' Lotte interrupted to remind her that it was more noted for Nazi rallies, the infamous Nuremberg laws, and if the world now looked at Nuremberg, it surely wasn't because of its toys and *Lebkuchen*, but to see the war criminals tried. Paul refused to discuss it and that made Lotte jump up and shout, 'Don't you think that the men responsible for the deaths of eleven million people in concentration camps alone should be tried?' Paul replied that she found it repulsive to see honorable men tried as common criminals.

"Lotte yelled, 'Mass murderers!' The class screamed, 'Our soldiers are as honorable as theirs, and concentration camps are a lie!' Can you imagine that they say that *after* the Auschwitz movie, the pictures and accounts in the papers? Anyway, when Lotte countered that German soldiers had raped, plundered, and burned villages, they all took it as personal insults to their fathers. There was pandemonium. I did my best, but what could I say? And I couldn't shout or argue, as Lotte did. But then no one listened. They all just shouted, yelled, and screamed, and it was Dr. Paul and the class on one side and Lotte and me on the other. You see, if it weren't for traitors like Lotte and me, Germany would have won the war."

"I know," Rolf said. "I've already heard it all, backward and forward. So then what happened?"

"We went to see Lotte's father. He was still working at

163

the Communist Party headquarters here. There must have been at least a dozen people there, and some had been in concentration camps. Of course, they were appalled that someone like Dr. Paul was allowed to teach. They debated for hours. Finally everyone agreed that we should send a written report to the school administration. We did, and we both signed it and took a copy to our director. She's a nice lady, and it upset her.

"Two weeks later the superintendent of schools arrived. A limp, oily washcloth of a man. He stood in front of the class and said, 'I've received an anonymous letter regarding certain remarks of Dr. Paul.' He said *anonymous* and was holding the letter with our signatures in his hand! The rest of what he said couldn't be heard because the whole screaming, shouting class turned on us with pointed fingers. He just stood there, helplessly waving his hands, and then— left, just left.

"We confronted him in the director's office, and you know what he said? 'I meant well. Didn't want to get you into trouble by mentioning your names.' Can you beat that? He also was astounded, that's the word he used, astounded that Paul not only had not denied having made those remarks but had insisted on repeating them. 'Most unfortunate,' he called it.

"Meantime, our dear classmates were arming themselves with stones and were waiting for us outside on the street. Lotte agreed to lie low only because I was so scared. When we didn't come out, they left and decided to give us the cold shoulder instead. But now that Lotte is gone, they have only me to ignore. That I don't mind."

"What happened to Dr. Paul?"

"She's out, allowed to teach only grade school."

"Disgusting. The military governments have ruled that no one who's been a member of the Nazi Party or its affiliates can be a teacher, judge, store owner. But what good does that do when it's impossible to fulfill this regulation? There simply aren't enough competent antifascists to fill all the positions in public life. Most either emigrated or died in concentration camps. My mother is right when she says she isn't sure whether it pays to have been for Hitler, but she's certain it doesn't pay to have been against him."

"I'm against Hitler and war, and I'm also tired of hearing about them. It's all so ugly. I long for beautiful things and for spring and art school."

"Do you know that the art academy is located right next to my conservatory? Tilla, we'll be able to see each other every day! Right now I have another idea. If you can boil some water, we'll make us a cup of coffee or cocoa."

"Coffee? Cocoa? We only have linden tea."

"My love! I came laden with gifts for you and your aunt Liz."

"Don't call her that!" she said, and looked away because he was getting out of bed. Then she stole a quick glance to see what he was doing. He went to his bag by the door. Mustering her courage, she watched as he bent down for it, was still watching him when he turned and came back. He smiled happily, knelt in front of her cot, and slowly put package after package on the blanket before her. There was coffee and cocoa, two chocolate bars, a pound of flour, and a can of meat.

When Elizabeth came home, all was in order, and they were both in the kitchen, watching the thin soup heat up. Though Rolf was in a hurry to leave, he stayed long enough to share it with them. No sooner had the door closed behind him when Tilla asked eagerly, "Do you like him? Isn't he nice?"

"Nice? I suppose so," Elizabeth answered without enthusiasm. "He certainly isn't much to look at."

"You don't think so?" said a surprised Tilla. "I think he's beautiful—and nice!"

"That's because you wear rose-colored glasses."

"Look at all this!" Tilla persisted. "Nice is hardly the word to describe his bringing us all these wonderful things."

"Generous is the word. Very generous indeed. He obviously has a crush on you."

"And I on him. I love him!"

"Tilla, at your age love is like a common cold. You catch it easily and it's over fast. You're too young for a serious involvement. He has no manners! The way he draped himself over the chair, legs half across the room. I didn't like that at all. That's all right when you kids are among yourselves, but not in my presence. I hope that when you do get involved, it will be with someone better than a bar musician. That Deemeetree! He was handsome *and* a gentleman. He would have been someone for you. Too bad he was a Russian."

166

28 "I found it!" Elizabeth said triumphantly. "Macdonnell of Glengarry—it's one of the oldest clans. There's even a picture of the tartan." Keeping a finger in the book, she regarded her niece. "You look very nice. The maroon dress certainly looks better on you than it ever did on Paula. But those shoes!"

Tilla's smile faded. "I don't have any others."

"I wonder," said Elizabeth before she left the room, then returned with a pair of beige pumps. "Maybe they'll fit you. Try them on."

Tilla carefully put them on. "They are beautiful! The leather is so soft, and they fit. But I can't wear these. What if something happens to them?"

"Nonsense," said her aunt, watching with a satisfied smile as Tilla, after a few cautious steps, walked back and forth with increasing assurance. "They're very becoming. High heels always make legs look longer and slimmer—not that that's something you have to worry about." She paused, then muttered, "I still don't like the idea of your being out so late and much less your staying overnight. I have never even met his mother."

"E-li-za-beth!" Tilla moaned. "Please don't start that again. It's almost seven. Jerry will be here any minute."

"Whoever he is," grumbled Elizabeth.

Tilla was so excited she couldn't remember whether or not she had put the keys in her bag and had to unpack it for the third time. But who wouldn't be? She was going to see Rolf again after what seemed an eternity. He was too busy studying during the day and playing at night. He might as well live on the moon rather than only in the center of Berlin. January had been thirty-one long, lonely days and nights, during which he had found time to send one postcard. February had been even worse; no word from him at all until, on March 8, his invitation had arrived.

> Meet me Saturday night in Bathtub (March 16).
> Jerry will pick you up around seven in the eve-
> ning. Going to party at American colonel's villa
> afterward, so you'll have to stay over. Edith
> wants to meet you!!! And I can't wait to see you
> again, my Tillangel. Regards to Elizabeth.
>
> Love,
Your Rolf

It would never have occurred to her that her aunt might object, and she was very surprised and angry when Elizabeth cited a hundred reasons why she couldn't possibly allow her to go. She finally, reluctantly, gave her consent partly because Major Macdonnell had told her that as far as he knew, and he was well informed in these matters, he said, no young girls had been sold into white slavery from the Bathtub. The Bathtub was, he said, a rather reputable place, as these places went, a jazz cellar and cabaret where mostly students gathered. The main reason Elizabeth gave her blessings, such as they were, was that she knew nothing could stop Tilla.

Jerry turned out to be an American lieutenant. He was tall and thin, in his late twenties, and had a pencil mustache. He smiled a lot, said little, and drove the rickety jeep like a madman through the dark, almost-deserted streets. Nothing could have fitted Tilla's exuberant mood more perfectly than this fast, bouncy ride. After taking the last corner on two wheels, they screeched to a sudden stop in front of an ordinary door, lit by a bare light bulb—the entrance to the Bathtub.

They could hear the noise even outside, but inside, it was deafening—and as dark as a cave. Small red lamps showed wafting clouds of blue cigarette smoke, gave just enough light to see that the place was packed. Hardly larger than an oversized living room, it held 200, maybe 300 applauding, foot-stomping, whistling young people jammed in, all the way to the door.

Jerry shouldered his way through the crowd, and a suddenly very nervous Tilla followed in his wake, climbing behind him onto the small darkened stage. It was the only sensible way to get to the other side, where they found bass, drums, the piano, and Rolf, surrounded by an agitated group. He was playing, but when he noticed her, he smiled and held up his cheek to be kissed. She did and jumped as he quickly pinched her. At that moment a blinding spotlight hit the stage. She stepped back, wedging herself between those standing there already, only two feet behind him. Onstage a young man announced, "Here she is, ladies and gents. The one you've been waiting for! IRENE WISTER!" Applause broke like waves crashing ashore as Irene, in a

low-cut red velvet gown, sidled up to the microphone. Tilla
craned her neck to see better. When Rolf began to play,
Irene seemed puzzled, looked in his direction, and gave a
short shrug, as if to say, "All right, if that's what you want,"
and began to sing in English:

> You'd be so nice to come home to,
> You'd be so nice by the fire. . . .

She had a rich, dark, and alluring voice:

> While a breeze, on high,
> Sang a lullaby,
> You'd be all that I
> Could desire. . . .

Forgetting all around her, Tilla wished she were up there
singing those words to Rolf.

> Under stars, chilled by the winter. . . .

Images of herself with Rolf flashed through her head.

> Under an August moon, burning above,
> You'd be so nice,
> You'd be Paradise
> To come home to and love.

Someone had put her feelings into words and music.

She was proud that she understood. *Thank you, Aunt Elizabeth*, she thought gratefully, *you are right to make me study English. I will tell her*, Tilla vowed. Her eyes were riveted on Irene, on her black, flashing eyes and sensuous movements. She watched the blood red nails stroking the mike suggestively. Irene moved to the edge of the stage, followed by the spotlight, and stepped down, singing:

> I should be excited,
> But Lothario, why not own up . . .

Now she leaned on the piano, over Rolf, revealing a considerable part of her white breasts, and she sang to him alone:

> That you always chase
> After ev'ry new face
> In town?
> I would be delighted
> If we two could, some day, be sewn up
> For if you behaved like a grown-up
> And could only slow down . . .

Tilla felt the blood rush to her face. What right had that Irene to be so close, so intimate with Rolf? *I'm jealous.* Tilla suddenly knew what the word meant. She was ashamed of herself but nevertheless relieved when the seductive Irene went back onstage and finished with:

171

You'd be Paradise
To come home to and love.

Applause and whistles. Lights went on. "Intermission!"

A crowd had gathered around the musicians. A solid wall of people now separated her from Rolf. And from the way they talked and joked, it was obvious that they all knew one another. In the center of things, where she knew Rolf to be, were Irene and another, very attractive girl with a long mane of hair, who squealed, "Aren't you the one, Severin! Just the boy I'd want to bring home to Mother!" Everyone laughed. Tilla didn't think it funny at all. He had said, "I can have more women than I'd know what to do with," and she had thought he was bragging.

She wondered whether to step in, somehow join the happy group, when Jerry materialized and pulled her to a nearby table, nudged her into an empty chair, and said, "Might as well sit down, babe. It'll be a while before sonny boy can dislodge himself. Want a beer?" He disappeared before she could answer.

"You Tilla?" A girl in a black turtleneck sweater and pageboy haircut asked and, when Tilla nodded, added, "Thought so. I'm Kovack." She sat down across from Tilla and pointed to the group around the piano. "Don't let that bother you. You'll get used to it. Mine's in there, too. Keep 'em happy in bed, always be around, but pretend not to be, that's what they like—that's the rule. Stick to it if you want him bad enough. You gotta want those crazy guys pretty damn bad." She gave Tilla a pitying look and explained,

"It's a lousy life, Tilla! Night after night in this or some other stinking hole. And when they're through, that's when they really get going. Can't ever get 'em to bed—I mean, sleep! There's always another party. When you're falling off your feet, that's when their genius hits 'em," she said with a sneer. "That's when they have to try out that new little riff, another world-shaking arrangement of Jerry's. He'll insist on it. As if they needed urging! They love it, and naturally, he's in seventh heaven. Little ol' musicologist Jerry has his own private combo to play every damn arrangement he concocts when he's on duty. Must do it on duty since he spends every other minute with them. They just about worship him, say he's the next Paul Weston or Sy Oliver. Yeah, don't underestimate our Jerry. He may not look it, but he's worse than the rest of 'em." Kovack laughed. It was a hoarse, throaty sound.

"You don't have to listen to me; you'll find out for yourself soon enough. But of course, with the two of you, it's all still roses and honey, rainbows and serenades. What a sweet, bloody, darling thing to do, 'You'd be so nice to come home to'!" Kovack made it sound ridiculous and saccharine-sweet.

"What do you mean?"

"Aw, come on! That's *your* song, isn't it? He played it when you came in, threw Irene a little curve there. When they're in the right mood, they do these little loving numbers. It sure wasn't on tonight's menu, I can tell you that!"

Jerry and the announcer joined them at the table. "Philip Anton Peters," said the announcer. "Honored to make your

173

acquaintance, my dear." He took her hand and kissed it with excessive flourish, while his eyes gave her a thorough once-over. "At last our doubts are laid to rest. There is a Tilla after all." He smiled.

"Flip can't help it." Kovack shrugged. "He was born with a mouth full of curlicues."

"Oh, daughter of Terpsichore! Why do you malign me so?"

"See what I mean?" said Kovack.

"Make room and stop bitching." It was the long-haired girl, who now pushed herself onto the chair with Kovack and asked, as though Tilla weren't there, "Rolf's new flame?" Then, facing her, she said with a strange smile, "Hello there, Rolf's new flame."

"Hello," said Tilla, and then Flip introduced her to Arnie, a boy with thick glasses and a pouting lower lip. There was Jan, who looked ascetic and seemed to belong to Kovack, and a Harald something, square-jawed and older than the others, and suddenly with great relief, she felt the gentle pressure of two hands on her shoulders.

"My angel," Rolf said into her ear, "did you like the song? Are you having a good time?" She nodded, wanted to answer, talk to him, but Irene was staring at her from two feet away. They were surrounded, locked in by the whole noisy group that had been at the piano.

Jerry stood so close that every time he leaned over, his uniform buttons touched her cheek. They did now, as he pushed empty glasses and ashtrays aside to make room for a piece of paper, which he laid down in front of her. "Rolf!

174

I want you to look at this!" Tilla bent forward so that Rolf could see better. "After the opening chorus you now have a descent from a high B flat," said Jerry. "Harald, Harald!" he yelled. Harald came over. They all leaned over her, fingers stabbing at the scribbles on the paper. "Harald," said Jerry, "you'll leap in on bar eighteen. I've changed things around a bit. The sequential treatment starts after the rest in bar twenty-seven. I've rewritten the whole goddamn arrangement. Will you guys try it?"

Tilla heard Rolf say, "Sure," as he pulled her earlobe. "All right by me."

"OK," said Harald, "but what about Jan?"

"His solo is self-contained. He'll ride with the rest," Jerry answered.

Rolf's voice again: "What's this, even-numbered beats?"

"Yeah, for four measures."

Irene and the long-haired girl were staring at her. *You can look all you want*, Tilla thought. *He's mine!*

Someone clapped; others joined in; soon the whole place shook to the shouts of "Jazz! Ami jazz! We want Ami jazz!"

When the lights went out completely, there were boos and shrieks. A kiss on the ear from Rolf. "We'll leave before the next set is over, angel."

The red lights came on again. Moments later only Kovack, Arnie, and Tilla were left at the table.

Flip, onstage with the mike, was picked up by the spotlight as he announced, "On bass—Harald Ammler!" Clapping and stomping over twanging of strings. "On drums— Jan Damman!" Drum roll to cheers and applause. "And on the keyboard"—Rolf ran his finger down the scale—"the boy wonder. Wonder boy!" Flip accelerated his speech; the name became almost a scream: "Rolf Andreas SEVERIN!" The audience went wild, hooted, stamped their feet, clapped, and whistled.

Jerry, by the piano, tapped his foot. At his signal the three instruments started as one. The music swept the audience along; they swayed in rhythm, tapped feet and fingers to the beat, screamed, "Do it! Go to it, Severin! Come on, let's hear it, Damman!" the crowd urged, as if the musicians were running a race.

Tilla was captivated, entranced, inside the music and so close to Rolf she could have touched him if she'd wanted to —Rolf, whose fingers produced this magic so new to her, yet already familiar. Ears, heart, soul, skin—all of her listened, rejoiced, began to identify phrases, recognized their return and paraphrasing. She was aglow, wanted to draw it, paint it, write about, shout, let it never, ever end.

Kovack smiled at her. She took the offered cigarette. Roll of drums, Jan's solo. Arnie got up, lit her cigarette, leaned over, and said something to Rolf, who slid off the stool as quickly as Arnie sat down on it. Rolf beckoned her to follow him through a side door.

In a narrow corridor she caught up with him. They embraced and kissed between stacks of empty boxes, piled-up chairs. A mass of chilly air hit them when the outside door opened and Jerry said impatiently, "Oh, come on, kids! Not now! We're late already."

Night wind blowing hair, crazy, bumpy ride. Jerry and

176

Rolf shouting, trying to hear each other over the engine, wind and squealing tires.

"What do you think?"

"What?"

"The bridge! Did you like the bridge?"

"Some shifty beat pattern, you bastard!"

"What?"

"I said you are a tricky bastard to write those beat patterns!"

"You bet!" Jerry yelled, and honked the horn one/two, one/two, one/two/three for emphasis.

Rolf held her tight; his hand, snuggled into her coat, cupped her breast, caressed it. She pressed her own bony frame against his—and was deliciously, deliriously happy: a modern princess in the arms of her prince, riding in a calèche to their brightly lit castle.

Lanterns around the driveway cast their light on many shiny limousines, staff cars with foreign military symbols. The drivers, fuzzy shadows, stood out of range of light, their cigarettes glowing in the dark. One coughed as they climbed the steps to the entrance.

A baby-faced MP, helmet strap cutting into his chin, opened the door. A maid in black dress, white cap, and apron took their coats, hung them on a rack already overflowing with heavy olive and khaki uniform coats, and there were a few furs among them. The MP's white-gloved hand received Jerry's cap, laid it on the shelf next to the others. An amazing row of stiff-crowned, visored officer's caps. Only the black kepis of the French were easily dis-

177

tinguishable. The American, British, and Russian ones varied little in color and shape, just in their cockades and braided cords. The MP opened the double doors to the main hall.

The vastness and splendor dazzled her: the sparkling crystal chandeliers, the Oriental rugs with their rich colors. The wide staircase which led to a gallery above was fit for a queen to descend. Its banister described a wide arc at the bottom, as if to embrace the grand piano standing there. What thrilled her most were the flower arrangements everywhere, enormous china vases filled with an abundance of lilacs, tulips, and exotic blossoms. *This*, she thought, *is my idea of a mansion.* She was glad now to be wearing a dress and high heels. In the Bathtub she had never even taken off her coat, feeling out of place with everyone else in sweaters and slacks.

Maids balancing trays with champagne glasses wove their way through groups of smoking, talking officers in dress uniforms. The few ladies among them looked very elegant in their long gowns.

"You look very beautiful, my Tilla!" Rolf said as one of the ladies came toward them. She was a small woman. Her gray silk gown matched the color of her short, curly hair and flowed around her slim figure. Her face was merry, full of wrinkles, yet stunningly beautiful. She slapped Jerry's arm in a friendly way.

"Happy to see that you all got here in one piece. Bar is to the left. I'm sure you'll find it." She laughed and flung her arms around the surprised Tilla, kissed her on both cheeks. "I'm glad you could come, Tilla. I'm Mary Schencke. I invited you." She turned to Rolf. "You're right! She does look like a picture. Very good. She'll make the dull brass shine." Mary put one arm around her, the other around Rolf, pulled them together, and confided, "Those military types are awfully dull, most of them anyway. You'll have to help me, Tilla. I count on you to get them away from their dreary battle talk. I, and the other ladies present, want to dance."

Tilla didn't have a chance to interrupt her to say that she didn't know how to dance. Mary continued talking rapidly. "Rolf, I'm afraid tonight you'll have to sacrifice art on the altar of shallow entertainment. You'll play those nice-and-easy no-strain-on-the-brain dance tunes for your old friend Mary, won't you?"

"Mary, you know," Rolf answered with a glint in his eye, "there's nothing I wouldn't do for you."

"You're lucky, Tilla. I won't put him to the test," Mary replied. "Thank God I'm a happily married woman." And as if she were reading Tilla's thoughts, Mary added, "Aside from the lamentable fact that I'm old enough to be his mother."

"That wouldn't stop me," said Rolf. "Not with someone as enticing, as gorgeous as you are."

Mary giggled, then quickly and expertly steered them past those assembled, used her foot to kick open the swinging kitchen door, and called out, "Here they are, Elise," and said to them, "Darlings, enjoy your dinner. See you in a while."

As soon as she was gone, Tilla said, "Oh, Rolf, she's wonderful!"

"I knew you'd like her," said Rolf. "She's an extraordinary woman. If it weren't for you, Tilla"—he grinned mischievously—"she'd be worth a sin—or two!"

"If you'd like your head shot off by the colonel," Elise remarked, putting plates, heaped with steaming food, before them. "He absolutely adores her."

Tilla would have liked nothing better than to sit by the piano with Rolf. But since she couldn't very well do that, she had hoped to hide behind the flowers there. But Mary's eagle eyes spotted her. She came and took her by the hand, walked her from group to group, introducing her with the happy pride of a mother.

Tilla was very much aware that she was the only young girl and, aside from Rolf, the only German at this party of the victors. It was Mary's strong grip on her hand, her warmth which enveloped her like a protective coat, that gave her confidence to face all these captains, majors, lieutenant commanders, brigadier something-or-others. They were very nice and polite to her, some openly flirtatious, as Mary was quick to point out. The ladies, however, were different. They acknowledged the introduction coolly, if not with open disdain. Mary squeezed her hand comfortingly when a tall, skinny blonde ostentatiously turned to avoid meeting her. Once out of earshot, Mary said, "Take it as a compliment, Tilla. She's jealous. You are beautiful and young, and she isn't." She handed her a glass of champagne, took another for herself. "Her husband is an RAF wing commander, not a bad-looking chap. He must have been drunk when he married her." She giggled. "Her voice alone would be enough to drive me nuts. But now, my dear, you *must* meet the colonel." She pulled Tilla into the adjacent room. "See! That's where all the men are. I should have known. Where else but at the bar?"

The colonel came to meet them. A big bear of a man, he made Mary look even smaller, more fragile. She introduced Tilla as Rolf's girl, and he said, "Aren't you a doll!" smiling at her appreciatively.

"Isn't she, though?" Mary agreed. "Bob! You have to help me break up this debating club. I want them to dance. I want a party!" She drew Tilla to an alcove where about twenty officers were engaged in intense conversation. Mary stopped one of the maids, nodded her head in the direction of the alcove, and said, "Make sure that there is enough vodka over there." To Tilla she said, "If we can get those Russians to dance, we'll be in business. There's one in particular that I have my eye on." She clapped her hands. "Gentlemen! Gentlemen!" Those closest to her turned. She stepped between them, dragging Tilla after her. "Gentlemen!" she said again as if making an important announcement. "The war is over! Rejoice! Be merry!" Those addressed didn't look at all happy at the interruption. Two even kept on talking, but Mary was not to be stopped. "This is not one of your conferences," she said almost petulantly. "I want this to be a party! And the ladies present wish to dance. Will you kindly oblige them? But before you all rush

181

off, I'd like you to meet my friend Tilla, a lovely young art student." Polite nodding of heads by some, continued conversation by others, as she rattled off their names and ranks. *Miraculous*, Tilla thought, *how she remembers it all.*

The last group of stubborn debaters stood by a window. The French officer in their midst tapped those around him on the shoulder, forced them to turn as she and Mary approached, and then her mind went blank and her heart stopped beating as she looked once again into those incredible deep blue eyes.

"Captain Gorchakov." Mary's voice came from far away. Dmitri bowed, said nothing, gave not the slightest indication that he had ever seen her before. "Captain Gorchakov!" Mary repeated. "May I count on you for a dance?"

"With pleasure, madam," he answered, taking her arm and leading her away.

Tilla desperately wanted, needed to be alone; but the French officer had asked her to dance, and he wouldn't take no for an answer. He moved smoothly, guided her so expertly that she only stepped on his foot twice. She excused herself as soon as the tango was over, but at once found herself on the arm of a white-haired, mustachioed gentleman, who proceeded to twirl her around to a waltz. Every time she tried to get away there was someone else demanding to dance with her. She danced with a wheezing old Russian, a smart, tall Englishman who squeezed her, Americans, French, and British, waltzes, tangos, and fox-trots between hasty sips of cool champagne, until people and things began to blur.

Pink-tiled bathroom. Powder room, the maid called it.

Tilla, still out of breath, looked at the radiant young woman in the mirror, a face both familiar and strange. Thought: *This is me.*

She stood very still, as all the impressions of the last hours began to whirl around her. Sentence fragments, sounds, and images turned cartwheels in her head, refusing to be caught, examined, put in order. Some, like Irene's red nails on the mike, flashed only once, disappeared with the speed of lightning. Others, like Mary's laughter, Rolf's voice, recurred, and always Mitya's eyes. *How*, she wondered, *would it feel to sleep with him?* That she was capable even of the thought startled her.

The door opened. Two middle-aged bejeweled ladies entered talking. "They are like animals, aren't they?" one said to the other. "But that blond one, I tell you! He could put his boots under my bed any day," Tilla heard as she closed the door behind her.

At the piano Rolf and Mary, to the obvious enjoyment of those gathered there, were playing a four-handed boogie. She went over to watch them. Rolf got up, embraced her, and quickly planted a kiss on her nose. She blushed when she saw that Dmitri, from the far corner of the room, was watching her.

The party was beginning to break up, and when Mary relinquished the piano to someone else, they said good-bye. She hugged and kissed them both, and Tilla had to promise to come visit her. "Since the good Jerry is three sheets to the wind, darlings," Mary said, laughing, "I'll have Paul drive you home."

"We'll be traveling in style," said Rolf as they climbed

into the plush limousine. The cushions were soft; the motor purred. It was warm, dark, and cozy. Her head on Rolf's shoulder, his arm around her, she listened to his voice, but the words didn't want to make sense . . . until she heard him call her name. "Tilla! Tilla! Wake up. We are home."

29

The hallway of the old apartment house was dark and smelled funny. A mixture of floor wax, cabbage, and something she tried, in vain, to define while they walked up the four flights of stairs. She felt strangely uneasy at entering this unknown apartment at night, having to tiptoe through rooms where she could dimly make out the contours of furniture.

"In here," Rolf whispered, guiding her through a door. She heard him close it. Then he switched on a light. "Welcome home, angel."

She didn't know what she had expected, only that it wasn't this utter chaos. There were books and sheet music stacked, helter-skelter, on the floor, all over the floor. They were heaped haphazardly on chair and desk and windowsill, ready to topple over any minute. In between were ashtrays full of butts, one sock, a wrinkled shirt—and a narrow, rumpled, none-too-clean, unmade bed. She suddenly felt trapped, wished for her own tidy room as he embraced her and whispered, "I've been wanting you so much, Till-

184

angel! Quickly, let's go to bed." And the urgency in his voice scared her.

"But where . . . do I sleep?" she asked, though she sensed what the answer would be.

"Here with me, of course!"

"But your mother!"

"My mother?" He laughed softly. "She's used . . . She doesn't mind. Believe me, she doesn't."

"But I do. I can't . . ." She clutched old Mr. Troester's bag, as if she could wring from it an answer about what to do next, and looked down at her feet in Elizabeth's pumps. "I can't," she whispered, "not with your mother here in the next room. What is she going to think of me?"

"Think? She's going to love you—because you're you! Tilla, you'll have to believe me. Edith is intelligent enough to accept the facts of life. She knows that people in love want to make love—or don't you? Anyway, the room next to mine is the hallway. Hers is at the other end. Does that make you feel better?"

When Rolf switched off the light, her eyes retained, for a while, what they last beheld: her neatly laid-out maroon dress on top of books, books, and books and Rolf. A naked, slender boy, who was already a man. The darkness was welcome, made her feel comfortable. It was good to be stretched out next to him, to snuggle up against each other. He caressed her tenderly until her longing matched his. *That's how it should be; that's how it would always be,* they assured each other as they fell asleep in each other's arms.

Morning found them, hand holding hand, still nestled into each other. They woke, turned to each other sleep-warm and drowsy, aware with intense pleasure of being together.

Later Rolf got a fat, old book with a worn leather spine. They sat up in bed, book on their laps, and flipped the pages of *The Picture Encyclopedia of Erotica*. Tilla, at first, didn't want to look, then alternately blushed and giggled. She was nevertheless relieved when he exchanged it for the huge Leonardo da Vinci volume. They quarreled then because he insisted on opening it to a certain page, and she wanted to start from the beginning. She gave in. Together they looked at the portrait of a young woman entitled "Lady with Ermine."

"That's the one," Rolf said excitedly. "Can't you see it? Admit it! She looks just like you."

"Maybe a bit . . ."

"Not maybe—definitely."

"A little bit."

"A lot!"

When they came into the living room, Rolf's mother was half leaning on the Steinway, reading a newspaper. Tilla saw a short woman with dark, curly hair. She wore a white blouse under a black pinstripe jacket and skirt. The severe lines of the suit made her look chubby, emphasized rather than hid the lack of waist and short legs. She had a strong, keen face and Rolf's eyes. But where his were warm, soft brown, hers had the deep color and hard sheen of a chestnut. Those eyes appraised her coldly, totaled her up as Tilla, shy and embarrassed, walked over to present herself.

"Rolf has told me a lot about you. I want you to feel at home here. Consider yourself part of the family," Edith said with warmth, though she made it sound like a command rather than an invitation. And she went back to her newspaper.

Tilla found her attractive but a bit scary, for Edith's presence far outweighed her physical shortcomings.

Professor Seewald held Tilla's hand for a long time between his freckled old ones, looked at her intently with pale, watery eyes. "Do you sing?" he had asked, and her reply that she didn't seemed to disappoint him. "You should sing *Lieder!*" he said more than once.

Rolf, using only one hand, played "Sah ein Knab ein Röslein stehn." "Try it," he urged. She shook her head and was glad that he didn't persist but sat down to play. "You'll like this one," he said. "It's called Concerto in Gusto Italiano. Bach wrote it in 1735 as part of—"

"It was *published* in '35," interrupted Professor Seewald. "He probably wrote it much earlier."

"Just listen to this four-bar sequence," said Rolf, playing it again.

"It's a true concerto grosso," lectured the professor, "composed for harpsichord alone." Rolf played, but Seewald went on. "Only on the double keyboards of a harpsichord with its varied registers. . . ." Rolf winked at Tilla and unexpectedly changed to syncopated 4/4 time. The professor shook his head and walked heavily across the

187

room. Before he went out, he turned once more, saying, "Have you no feeling left at all? After Bach to go to this . . . this whorehouse music!"

"Never fails," said Rolf. "Gets rid of him every time."

"Of me, too." Edith laughed, retreating to her room.

Tilla made her first, feeble attempt. "I ought to go home, Rolf." He smiled and played the song she wanted to hear. "You'd be so nice to come home to,/You'd be so nice by the fire." He talked over the music, and after that it was "What is this thing called love?" and then it was "Night and day, you are the one," many, many beautiful songs, and Tilla beamed with pleasure and forgot everything else, and Rolf kept on playing for her.

"Beats German coffeehouse music, *hm?*" he asked, immediately giving a rendition of a cloyingly sentimental song before coming back to the music he had started with. "You know, angel, that one piece, the Italian Concerto, will be part of my first concert." He stuck out his tongue toward Professor Seewald's room. "Of my *piano* recital." He played it again, and the shadow of the Steinway lay long and dark over the room. The day was fading.

She hated to have to say it: "Rolf! I really have to go home."

"Why? Why can't you stay here?" he demanded like a querulous child.

"Because my aunt—"

"Your aunt doesn't need you! I do. I do, I do, I do!" He stamped his foot like a naughty little boy. It was a silly argument, but they carried it to a point where she began to doubt her own reasons. What were they after all? Her aunt would miss her for a while but . . . Her room with the bicycle? She realized then that it was something else. She couldn't explain it, knew only that she had to go home. He finally gave in. "I'll walk you to the station."

They reached the station much too fast, couldn't part there, walked to the next one and then all the way to Zoo Station, where she could get a train directly to Hermsdorf. They missed the train and, since there would be an hour's wait, decided to go to the zoo across the street. It was mild for March; there was just a whiff of spring in the air as they walked hand in hand through the black-market crowd into the zoo.

They didn't have to pay. The ticket booth, like the rest, was in ruins. There were no animals. Still, it was a place to walk around and be alone.

"You should have seen it before the war," said Rolf. "It was beautiful. Look at the mosaics and arches over there. That used to be the elephant house. And when it happened, I was up there"—he pointed to the huge, ominous gray bunker that remained—"carrying flak ammo, when they bombed it. I saw bears trapped in their burning cages, and giraffes and antelopes running loose. They were crazed with fear, and so was I. It was terrible."

"I know," she said, remembering the charred leopard hanging in the tree. "It was that way in Dresden, too." Instinctively they drew closer together, hand gripped hand more tightly, as their memories served up those awful,

189

powerful images once again. This wasteland was no zoo; it was a giant chamber of horrors, and all too recent and real.

It was consoling, calming to see the first leaves of grass, weeds growing around the burned-out, broken war machinery, to watch sparrows and pigeons pick at ants in the shell-cracked pavement. But then they saw the two emaciated horses with scabby skins like moth-eaten fur. At the first sight of Tilla and Rolf, the horses came to the fence, one loping, the other limping. They stood swinging their heavy heads to and fro, to and fro, occasionally baring large yellow teeth. The limping horse had only one good eye; the other was swollen shut. They stood looking at Rolf and Tilla with three big, sad, accusing eyes.

"I'm sorry," Tilla said, helplessly holding up her empty hands. "I have nothing for you. I'm sorry."

"Poor beasts," she heard Rolf say. "Look! He's crying! His one eye is crying."

"I can't stand it!" Tilla wailed, tears running down her cheeks. He pulled her away, but she saw that he, too, was crying. Looking neither left nor right, they ran all the way back to the station . . . and, because they couldn't part that way, went into the station restaurant.

It was a dimly lit place, smoke-filled, figures crowded around the bar, bodies in many layers of clothing, frayed blankets over army coats of many hues. But all and everything looked gray under the filter of the evil-smelling smoke of homegrown tobaccos, hand-rolled cigarettes filled with remnants of stubs. A haggard soldier leaned against the wall, one empty trouser leg folded, held up by safety pins, his coat tied together with string. On the floor, by his one foot, a pile of blankets, from which only the withered face of an old man or woman peered out. Bony fingers clutched a paper bag. Wherever she looked, thin gray faces, dead eyes, except for those of the shadowy men, who flitted through the crowd, now here, now there, never long in one spot. The black marketeers had alert eyes, alert, darting, cold, and greedy.

"This used to be a really clean place," she heard Rolf say. "Even during the war. You should have seen those sparkling counters with mouth-watering displays of sandwiches and cakes. They had white tableclothes on all the tables and . . ."

To Tilla it looked like an overcrowded asylum for the unsheltered, catchbasin for what the war had spit out. They were the broken, the derelicts, cretins, all the monstrosities that in normal times avoided the light of day. This ragtag crowd leaned, crouched, lay about in a seemingly noncaring stupor. A Hieronymus Bosch nightmare.

Rolf had spotted an empty chair, dragged Tilla to it. He held it until she was seated. The old man sitting at the table got up, offered his place to Rolf, and disappeared before they could protest. There they sat, looking at each other across the dirty table, wet rings from glasses that had been removed, a crumpled empty cigarette package, which Rolf flicked to the floor.

Two women, blond, color out of bottles, with bright red lipstick, dislodged themselves from the bar and came sauntering over. They wore, under their open coats, very

191

short skirts. The garter showed when the taller one ostentatiously scratched her leg a few inches from Rolf's face. They stared coldly at Tilla. *This is our turf,* they seemed to say, *don't get ideas.*

"Students!" said the short one in disgust before they turned to go back to the bar.

"I'm sorry, Tilla! In normal times I would have taken you to the Adlon Hotel. Roses on every table, crystal glasses, champagne . . ."

"It's all right."

"You are cold."

"No, I'm not."

"Maybe we can get something to eat. . . ."

A sour-looking waiter appeared, glared at them as he wiped his hands on a dirty towel. "Beer-seltzer-toddy?" he rattled off.

"Two toddies, please, and would you have anything to eat?"

"Soup—one meat coupon."

"No," said Rolf, "I mean, without coupons . . . maybe for a few . . ." but the waiter was already gone. "Oh, Tilla!" Rolf sounded as helpless as he felt in the face of the dirt, the stench, the cold, and the hunger. "If only it were summer!"

"Yes, if only it were summer," echoed Tilla.

"You know what we'd do if it were summer?"

"What?"

"We'd drive to our country place and go for a swim in

the lake, and after that we would have lunch on the terrace—"

"The terrace is always so drafty."

"Under the birches then?"

"Yes, I like that. But have Otto bring the striped um-
brella. It's getting hot."

"You're right. I can see the air shimmer, and look at
those white, puffy clouds. You see the one over there?"
They both looked at the dirty ceiling, where a single naked
light bulb hung on a wire. "Doesn't it look like a dragon?"

"It does," said Tilla. "A dragon, but now it's changing
into a dinosaur."

Then the dinosaur faded away, was once more nothing
but a peeling, dirty ceiling. Rolf put his arm around her
shoulder. "Guess the waiter has forgotten us." Tilla jumped
up in panic.

"Oh, my God! Rolf! What time is it! I have to go!" And
she ran to the exit so quickly that he had trouble following
her. Together they sprinted up the stairs to the railroad
platform. The train was there.

He had only time to ask, "Next Saturday? Will I see you
again? Will you come?" when the electric doors closed between them. The train started, accelerated. *She did nod yes,*
Rolf told himself, *she did nod yes.*

30 The streets were still wet from a passing shower. It had left the air fresh and smelling of spring. Friday, April 12, 1946. Had anyone ever longed so much for a day? Tilla walked quickly through the gate of the art academy. One week ago she had brought her portfolio here—two pieces of black cardboard, hinged by a strip of gray linen. There were ties at the top, bottom, and on the side to hold her sketches, watercolors, designs—the thirty best ones, painstakingly picked out of the many she had done. A ray of late-afternoon sun hit the brass doorknob just as she reached for it. *That has to be a good omen,* she thought as she stepped through the door.

The office was to the right and open. The middle-aged woman behind the typewriter studied her nails. She yawned as Tilla came in and said a long, drawn-out "Yes?"

"I would like to find out if I've been accepted."

"Nobody's been accepted. They've only decided who's allowed to take the exam. Did you leave a portfolio?"

"Yes."

The secretary got up reluctantly. "Name?"

"Wenkenberg. Tilla Wenkenberg," she answered, looking with pounding heart at the hundreds of portfolios on the long table behind the secretary. They were three distinct groups. The largest to the left, in the center a stack of ten, maybe fifteen, and on the right, a pile of about eighty.

She had worked so hard to get hers together that there

had been neither time nor room for doubt. But now, as she watched the secretary flip through the stacks, her confidence evaporated. *What,* she thought, feeling panic set in, *if they don't take me? I'll have no choice but to do another year, one hell of an eternity at Hermsdorf High.*

"What color is it?" the secretary asked, furtively scratching her thigh through the tight skirt.

"Black," she answered, "with a red dot on the back, I mean spine," she quickly corrected herself. The red dot had been a heart pasted on, for good luck, by Rolf. It had not been easy to convince him that in this case a circle would be more appropriate.

"Here we are," the secretary announced, pulling it from the center pile and putting it on the desk before her. She took off the attached note. "It says here," she read, " 'Advise to come back next year. You're too young.' " Tilla's heart sank. "But—you're allowed to take the exam if you want to. I don't know why they do that." She shook her head with obvious disapproval. "No point to it, is there? This art academy is the only one with university status," she said, with pride, "which means you *have* to be eighteen and a high school graduate."

Tilla tried not to show her disappointment, tied the little cords with shaking hands. "When does the exam start, and what do I have to bring?"

"Monday morning, nine o'clock. Pad and pencil are all you need. But if you ask me, you'll just be wasting your time."

The portfolio tucked tightly under her arm, she walked

slowly down the marble steps. It couldn't be; there must still be a chance; all couldn't be lost. *Why allow me to take the exam when I don't have a chance?* She was glad that she hadn't told Elizabeth, had wanted to wait until she could announce to her that she was officially enrolled, so at least she would be spared her derision. Her aunt had little interest in her drawings, was firmly convinced that she should become an interpreter ("with your wonderful ability for languages . . . rare gift, interesting life, international flavor . . . meet the right kind of people").

She fought back her tears and thought of Rolf and her friends at the Bathtub. The Bathtub had become her base, her home. She saw it now, in her mind's eye, as she would see it in half an hour—the scuffed black walls, the stage with the old lion-footed bathtub on it, all the empty chairs and tables, the piano, and the big case of Jan's bass behind it. Saw the cord and the microphone on its stand, every detail of the place that looked so shabby when it was empty. But once all the animated students crowded in, when the lights were turned low and the music began, it came alive. Then it was again the inspiring magical cave.

By the time she reached the back entrance she felt a little less depressed. Rolf and Kovack, Arnie and Flip would do the rest to lift her spirits.

"Hello, Tilla." Mr. Breyer, the fat manager, smiled as she passed him. In the storeroom, through which she had to go, Fritz was counting bottles, calling out the numbers to Karl, who wrote them down on a pad. The two waiters stopped to greet her.

"Pass the news, kid," Fritz said. "Good or bad?"

"Bad, almost," she replied. "They said that I'm too young, that I should come back next year . . . but they will let me take the exam. If I do well, do you think they'll make an exception?"

"For you? They will have to make an exception. Of course, they will," Karl declared. "You know, my old lady thinks your stuff is first-rate, and she knows about things like that. The picture you did of me? She loves it and is having it framed."

"Don't worry, they'll take you," Fritz agreed. "What's age got to do with talent anyway? When's the exam start?"

"Monday, and it lasts a whole week."

"Tilla! We'll keep our fingers crossed for you."

This vote of confidence, their approval of her pleased her very much. In the beginning they had shown her the professional insider's contempt for hangers on, but once she had started drawing, things changed. They had become her critics—always quick to point out when something wasn't right—and her admirers. She wondered what they did with all the sketches they so proudly carried away. *They like me and respect me,* she thought, *maybe not quite as much as Kovack, but then Kovack is Jan's wife and a soloist with the Hebbel Theater ballet—and very funny—my friend.*

She could hear them talking now. She peeked around the corner, caught Jan's eye. He promptly twanged "You'd be so nice to come home to."

"Artist's theme song!" Kovack called in her raspy voice. "Where is she?"

"Here I am," she answered happily. Rolf picked her up, hugged and kissed her, and they all crowded around. Kovack, Jan, Flip, Arnie, and even the tight-lipped Harald —everyone discussed her chances, agreed that with her talent an exception would surely be made. Her confidence returned with so much ego bolstering, and she felt warm and happy to have found such friends. Arnie squeezed her hand in his shy way, and when he looked at her with his soulful eyes, he seemed really to understand how much it meant to her, more so even than Rolf.

When Harald seated himself behind his drums and Jan picked up the bass, she took Rolf aside. "I have to go home."

"You're not leaving!" He was incredulous. "You just got here."

"I have to. My aunt doesn't even know I'm here."

"Why didn't you tell her?"

"You know why!"

"If you had told her, you could stay over."

"No. You know she'll allow it only on weekends, and then not very willingly. I promised to come let you know, and I did."

"You don't love me! Your aunt is more important to you than I am!"

"That's not fair! I do love you. I'm coming back tomorrow, and then I'll stay over. Tonight I'm going home."

"I need you, Tilla. I want you with me all the time."

"I want to be with you, too, but I also have things to do —work."

"You work here, don't you? Half of your portfolio are the sketches you've done here!"

"Sketches, sure. But you do more than finger exercises, don't you?" Her eyes blazed. "Or do you? You tell me that you're so darn busy practicing for that first concert that you can't even spare the time to come out and see *me!*"

"Tillangel! Why do you have to make everything so difficult?"

"I'm not the one who makes things difficult. You are! I can't just sit here night after night and adore you!" she said angrily, then had to laugh when she saw his big grin. "I mean," she said, "I have to do something besides that, or you'd get tired of me fast. I want to be more than a dumb schoolgirl, drooling over you. There are plenty of them around. Don't forget I see them, and I know what you think of them."

"You're not dumb. And I'll never get tired of you."

"Rolf!" she said, exasperated. "I can't be happy just hanging around. Can't you understand that?"

"Of course I understand. What I can't understand is that it always requires being away from me."

"I thought I explained that."

"Will you move in with me when you're accepted at the art academy?"

"If I'm accepted."

"Will you?"

"Rolf, I have to go. I don't want to miss the six o'clock train."

"We're just starting to go over the blues number."

"Arnie said he'd walk me to the station."

"You'll come back tomorrow and stay over?"

"I said I would. Good-bye, Rolf."

"Till tomorrow, Tillangel."

31 "It always seems to happen overnight," Elizabeth said, opening the door to the balcony. "Suddenly all the trees are green with leaves. It's a joy to see blue sky and sun, especially after the winter we've had. I think it's even warm enough to go without a coat."

Tilla looked out into the sunshine. Tomorrow she would know. She had been far too excited about the exam not to tell her aunt about it. Elizabeth, to her surprise, had encouraged her in a way by saying, "I'm glad you're taking it. That way you will know whether or not you have enough talent to make it a career. There is nothing so dismal, to my mind, as people who delude themselves into thinking that they are artists when they are at best bloody amateurs. I am sorry that I don't know enough to tell, but the professors at the academy ought to know. The sooner you find out, the better off you are. Believe me, you will save yourself a lot of unnecessary heartache."

Elizabeth tore yesterday's page from the calendar and

said, interrupting Tilla's thoughts, "Monday, the twenty-ninth of April. I must remember to pick up my shoes from the shoemaker tonight."

"I'll get them for you," Tilla offered.

"That would be nice. Then I don't have to rush, in case Major Macdonnell asks me to stay a little longer. It happens so rarely I'd hate to have to refuse."

You wouldn't, Tilla thought with understanding and amusement. *You'd stay even if all your shoes were at the shoemaker.* Aloud she said, "Don't worry, I'll be glad to."

"Isn't today the day you find out?" her aunt queried.

"Tomorrow," Tilla answered. "That is, I could find out today, except that Rolf has a late class and Wednesday is a holiday. That's why we thought tomorrow would—"

"I'd already be there!" Elizabeth interrupted her impatiently. "Why should you have to wait for Rolf to find out if the academy has accepted you? What does he have to do with it? If I were you, I'd be on my way," she said emphatically and looked at Tilla, who was still in her nightgown. "Well, I guess you won't be ready in time to take the train with me, so take the next, but by all means, find out today."

"I want to, only I was afraid you wouldn't allow me to go in two days in a row. You see, Rolf and the others are planning a kind of celebration tomorrow night."

"You can go, provided you come home afterward." She looked at her watch. "Dear me! I'd better run. I hope to hear good news tonight, Tilla. Really, I wish you luck. You may think I don't know how much you're counting on it,

201

but I do." She suddenly gave her an unexpected little kiss. "Good luck!"

"Thank you, Aunt Li . . . Elizabeth."

The suspense was so great that she had indeed thought about going in ever since she awakened. But she thought it would be unfair to Rolf. Now Elizabeth had helped change her mind. Her aunt was right. Why should she have to wait that long? No harm would be done if she found out today since she could meet Rolf, as planned, tomorrow. As a matter of fact, if she had been rejected, it would be better this way. She would be able to do her crying by herself. She didn't doubt for a second that she would cry. It was, however, a hopeful Tilla who boarded the nine o'clock train in Hermsdorf.

She was glad to be alone, rather than have to ride with her aunt. One and a half hours to think back on the most wonderful, most exciting, exhilarating, outrageously happy week of her life. Every single one of those five days had been an adventure, a battle to be fought. And at the end of each day there had been Rolf, comforting and assuring her that it would be won. She thought of the life class on the first day. There had been a male model. It had embarrassed her. Everyone else had set to work, without batting an eyelash; only she had blushed, and the professor had noticed it. He had come over and slapped her on the back—"You'll get used to it"—and that made it even worse. He was a short man with a shock of wild black hair, bushy eyebrows over steely eyes, which had seemed always to be on her. He wore a yellow shawl so long it trailed on the floor when he paced up and down like a caged lion. He had scared her, but it had helped some when he pointed to one of her drawings as an example of what he considered good.

He was, she found out, Stephanoff, the famous book designer and illustrator, notorious among the students for his harsh manner. She had fought for three days to get the forms and poses of the models on paper. Maybe it had been her imagination, but it had appeared that whenever she happened to look up, she met his eyes. It had made her concentrate twice as hard, so much so that she had even forgotten Rolf.

On the fourth day they had had to draw a still life with bottles and a perspective rendering of an ornate chair. She couldn't get it right, not even with the whispered instructions from the kind Professor Fisher. Her bottles had resembled cucumbers, and just thinking of the chair made her cringe. This had been the worst day of the five.

The written and oral tests had been given on Friday. She could still see the twelve venerable professors seated at the long table. They had fired questions at her, everything from German history to what kinds of books she read. To judge by their reaction, she had done well. No wonder. Rolf supplied her with the best literature, and the long train rides had given her ample time to read. It was also thanks to Rolf that she knew as much about art as she did.

He liked to look at art books with her. They often sat in bed, with two or more from Professor Seewald's extensive collection.

It was thrilling to think that she would have that all the time once she was married to Rolf. Wonderful to know in advance that it would be wonderful. Rolf, Rolf, Rolf. She couldn't imagine life without him. He had met her every day, had waited on the front steps of the academy, wearing the khaki jacket with a thousand pockets. As they walked, she had told him everything about her day, tried to imitate the other students, mimicked the professors, done the models' poses for him. He had liked that, and it had sharpened her observations. She was greatly pleased that she could make him laugh.

It took an hour, but each day they had walked all the way to the zoo and, starting at the gate, raced each other to Eduard and Kunigunde. The two poor, starved horses had allowed them to pet their heads after gobbling up whatever they brought them. From there they had walked to the rock mountain. It had been arranged and planted to resemble the natural habitat of bears. The bears were gone; only the plaque "Ursus arctos" remained, and a bench —a small bench, partially hidden in a niche. A lovers' place, perfect for a quick kiss, ideal for sitting close together and talking about love. A place where one wasn't ashamed to say all those silly nonwords that jump off the tongue because there is no other way of expressing what the overflowing heart feels. This had been the last good part. After that had come the walk to the station and parting. At that point the conversation had repeated itself each night. "Why can't you stay with me?" he would ask. "Why spend an hour on the train tonight when you'll have to do the same thing again tomorrow morning?"

Even Mrs. Severin ("call me Edith") had started to pressure her to come more often. "You are good for Rolf," she had told her. "A calming influence. He needs that! I can't wait for him to give that first concert, start his career, and settle down." She had given "settle down" a special emphasis.

As much as Tilla longed for that day, too, she knew that she needed time. There was so much to learn before she could get married. Now she had reached the entrance to the academy and pushed those troubling thoughts from her mind as she entered the office.

The dour secretary wasn't there. Instead, there was a nice young man, who asked her name. But it took a long time before he found it. Other students pushed in front of her. It was so noisy that she had to ask twice because she couldn't hear what he said. "Accepted," the young man said now, loud enough for everyone to hear. "You're accepted. Congratulations!"

"Oooh!" she cried, leaping into the air, making everybody laugh. They were still laughing when she ran out and jumped down the stairs. Then she remembered that she had forgotten to ask for particulars and had to go back.

"The semester starts next Monday, May the sixth," the young man informed her and, after checking a book, gave her an admiring glance. "You'll be in Stephanoff's class," he said as the students began to whistle. "You must be pretty darn good if *he* takes you."

Stephanoff's class! It scared her more than it pleased her. She would have much preferred kind Professor Fisher, but that was a small fly in the ointment. *Hurrah! I'm accepted!* she would have liked to shout. Instead, she did some pirouettes and threw her portfolio into the air. It was her lucky day—she caught it. She played hopscotch on the big concrete slabs of the sidewalk, hummed to herself: "You'd be so nice to come home to!" But with the art academy in mind, she changed the text to "You'll be so nice to go to." Go to? Go to where? Where should she go to now? Why, to Rolf, of course. He should be the first to know. He might still be at home. *If not, I'll go to the conservatory.* Her hair flew as she skipped along, smiling at everyone she passed.

She slowed down only on the last flight of stairs, and as she looked at the two nameplates, Prof. E. Seewald and below it, Dr. H. Severin, she suddenly felt uneasy. *Well,* she told herself, *if he isn't home, I'll tell Professor Seewald. He'll be happy for me, too.* But there was a little voice in her head that said: *You can't just march in uninvited. It isn't done!* . . . *Why not?* she answered it boldly. *They say I'm part of the family.* . . . *Not yet,* the little voice persisted. *One doesn't drop in on people at eleven in the morning. You know it isn't right. Where are your manners?* . . . *No one sleeps till eleven,* she answered it weakly and, fighting her feeling of apprehension, rang the bell.

There was no answer. She waited on the dark landing.

206

It had been sunny outside, and here it was gloomy. She rang again. Still nothing. She was about to give up when she heard footsteps, the slow, shuffling ones of the professor.

"Who is it?" he asked in a quavering voice.

"It's me, Tilla!"

"Who?"

"Tilla. Rolf's friend Tilla."

"Ah, yes," he mumbled. "Tilla."

She heard him fumble with the door lock and mutter to himself, thought he said that Rolf wasn't home, so she called out, "I just came to say hello, Professor Seewald. I've been accepted at the art academy!"

"Ah, yes, yes, yes, of course," he said, finally opening the door. He stood there without moving and looked at her strangely. "Very nice, very, very nice. I'm happy for you, Tilla. You deserve it. Congratulations. Do you want to come in?"

"Well," she said, taken aback because he usually greeted her with an affectionate hug. Suddenly she didn't know what to do. Why should he be so odd and distant, today of all days? She hesitated a moment, then said, "Thank you," and stepped forward. But she had to squeeze by, so reluctant was the professor to let her in. He hurried past her and insisted that she follow him into the kitchen, where he would make her a cup of tea, even though she told him three times that she didn't want any. *Rolf is right, he is getting senile,* she thought, as she watched him pick things up only to put them down in the same spots. He wouldn't allow her to help either, and his shaky hands rattled the cups and saucers.

"So how was it? Tell me, how it was?" he asked. "What exactly did they say?"

"They said I will be in Professor Stephanoff's class. You know, Stephanoff, the book designer? You showed me the *Gulliver's Travels* he illustrated. He's going to be my professor. Isn't that wonderful?"

"They didn't say anything about your age?"

"No."

"Very nice. Congratulations." He started to pour the hot water on the floor instead of into the teapot, and she barely prevented him from scalding himself. Never had she seen him so nervous and absentminded.

"Are you all right?" she asked, thinking: *What do I do if he has a heart attack?*

"I'm very well, very well indeed," he replied, handing her a cup and spilling half the tea.

"Let me carry it all in," she offered, reaching for the wicker tray she had handled so often.

"W-w-why? W-why . . . w-w-well, w-w-well, if-f-if-f-if-f y-you m-m-must," he stuttered, which she took to mean yes, though she sensed that something was wrong. *Maybe I should make him lie down*, she thought as she quickly loaded the tray and went on ahead through the familiar corridor. She went into the living room, where she placed the tray on the small table opposite the Steinway, its customary place.

And then Rolf's door opened. He stood there barefooted,

dressed only in his bathrobe, rubbing his eyes with his fists. He stretched, yawned—and saw her. Saw her and quickly closed the door behind him. Not quickly enough. She had seen her, the hair, the black, flashy eyes, the red nails dug into his blanket. Irene Wister was lying in Rolf's bed.

She understood in a flash the reason for Professor Seewald's behavior. She had been too deaf and blind in her happiness to grasp what any idiot would have instantly understood.

For one long moment Rolf and Tilla stood silently staring at each other. Then she ran into the corridor. He followed her, grabbed her hand. "Tilla! Please, Tilla, let me explain!"

"There's nothing to explain," she snapped.

"Tilla, please! It has nothing to do with us! Believe me! It means nothing! Tilla! Tilla!"

"Then I . . . what we did means nothing to you either!" she cried, shaking him off.

"Children! Please!" Seewald stammered, helplessly waving his arms.

Tilla picked up her portfolio, tugged at it, as Rolf had taken hold of it, too, succeeded in tearing it away from him, and ran out the door, down the stairs, followed by Rolf's pleading cries: "Tilla! Please come back, Tilla! Tilla! Wait!"

32 Arnold Steingasser was walking aimlessly down Grolmanstrasse. He had expected it, of course, but now that it had happened, it depressed him. They had actually thrown him out, expelled him from law school for nonattendance. "Poor, orphaned Arnie," he mocked himself. "Let's face it, you lack what it takes. You are and always will be Arnie, the vagabond, the tramp."

He had stopped to wipe his glasses and scrutinize Schiller's bar. It made him think of Rolf. *Always good for a laugh, that Rolf*, he thought, and decided to go over to Knesebeckstrasse to see whether he was home. He had just rounded the corner when, to his surprise, he saw Tilla. She seemed to come flying out of the house, then ran down the street. On an impulse he had followed her.

Looking to neither the left nor the right, she ran down Carmer, then Fasanenstrasse, crossed Steinplatz oblivious to the traffic. He hurried after her along Bismarck and Englischestrasse, watched her climb the huge mountain of rubble behind the burned-out porcelain factory. She clawed her way to the top, then crouched under a twisted girder. He was about to approach her but stopped when he heard her first, heart-rending sob.

Tilla, in total misery, had pulled her head down between her shoulders and was hammering her fists on her head. "Why? Why, why?" she wailed, wishing she could stop the vivid pictures her mind projected. But she couldn't, no matter how hard she pressed the heels of her hands on her eyes. Rolf in the hay shed, Rolf at the piano, Rolf in her room, on her bike, in her bed, Rolf, Rolf, Rolf . . . It was like a movie run by a mad projectionist, backward and forward, in and out of focus, freezing always at one particular frame. Irene, behind Rolf, in Rolf's bed. She would never see him again, never, ever again. . . . Even if he came crawling. She couldn't, not after what he had done. But never to be able to see him again made her emit loud, blubbering sobs. He had destroyed everything. They could never be happy again. He didn't love her. He was in love with beautiful, sophisticated, seductive Irene. Irene, the singer. She, Tilla, couldn't even carry a tune. How could she have been stupid enough to believe he could love her? *Admit it, Tilla. You are nothing, nothing at all, compared to Irene.* . . . "We'll get married right after my first concert." She had believed him. *Why did he do that to me?* She groaned. It was mean, rotten, devious, the way he had done it. He should have been honest and told her to her face. She hammered her fists with such fury on a brick that she bloodied her knuckles. It proved only that she wasn't dreaming. She had seen Irene in his bed. He had made love to Irene. If she hadn't barged in, she wouldn't have known, but she would have found out sooner or later. "Sooner is better. It saves unnecessary heartache," Elizabeth always said. Except it didn't. But it didn't matter because it was all over. Everything was over. It would have been nice to study art. But no more. There was no point to it or anything else.

Arnie kept his vigil from a distance. He had coughed, more than once, hoping that she would notice him. But she didn't, and he lacked the courage to disturb her. It was beginning to get dark when she finally got up, hurriedly descended, and headed for the Spree Bridge. She stared for a long time at the dark, dirty water, fifty feet below her, while he inched closer. He was about to call her name when she suddenly started running again. He raced after her, saw her enter Tiergarten Station. She was leaning over the edge of the platform.

Tilla looked directly into the headlights of the oncoming train; then, at the last second, as it thundered into the station, she drew back and at the same time was pulled from behind.

"There's no guarantee!" someone yelled into her ear. She wheeled around and faced Arnie. "It's not as foolproof a method, as one might assume," he said. "Might only lose a leg. This, however, will always assure you a seat *on* the train. You know, one of those reserved for cripples and pregnant women. Me! I'd rather be pregnant." He gently put his arm around her, took her portfolio, and walked her away from the train and the station. "People are very stupid." He tried to soothe her. "Even professors. Schubert's genius wasn't recognized either. They had to bury him in the cemetery for the poor. Did you know that?" She gave in to another noisy, crying fit. "It's not the end of the world, Tilla. It's only one year. What's one lousy year? It'll be over before you know it. They'll be happy to take you then, I'm sure."

212

"But it isn't that!" she said, sobbing. "I've been accepted at the academy. It isn't that!"

He didn't have to ask, he knew. He had seen Rolf and Irene whispering and leaving together. Anger rose in him at Rolf, who could do this to, of all girls, Tilla. Tilla, worth a hundred Irenes. *But that's how it is*, he thought, *Rolf has everything* and *Tilla—but that's not enough for him. He still has to go whoring. Why can't she love me? I would never be unfaithful to her. I'd do anything for this girl, if only she knew it, but she's crying her eyes out over Rolf, not me.*

He steered her into a dingy corner pub, led her to a booth. She didn't protest, sat down like an obedient child. He ordered two German vodkas and studied her. The lovely tearstained face, her fine hair, the kind of dark amber shade he liked. She sat hunched over and wept.

The waiter brought the two vodkas. At the bar three rough young workers were throwing dice. "Chicago," one called out, beating the leather cup hard on the counter. The middle one picked it up, shook it noisily. "Come on, let's see it, baby needs shoes!" He bent back, laughing, and his fist came down hard on the polished-from-use wood. "What did I tell you? Lehmann-wife-and-three-children! That's worth another round, Mack. Press 'em in!" While Mack filled the glasses, they were quiet, then turned and stared curiously at the weeping Tilla.

"You are putting me in a terrible position," Arnie said to Tilla, and smiled. "Anyone seeing us probably thinks I'm the cad who made you pregnant and now I refuse to marry you." He joked, hoping that she would react.

She tried to smile. "I'm sorry."

"It's all right. I don't care. As long as you're with me, I don't give a damn what anyone thinks." He handed her one of the glasses, took the other, and lifted it in a toast. "Here's to you, kid! Unburden yourself on my masculine shoulders. Tell your uncle Arnie, and all will be well."

"Uncle Arnie! That's ridiculous," she said. "You're only twenty-two."

"Twenty-three," he corrected her. "Six years older than you are, my dear. Six and one half years, four and a half of them fighting in the war. Count each of those years for ten. They've made me as old as the hills. And the hills have seen a lot and suffered a lot. Shall we try to drown our sorrows together?" They drank, and then she had started to talk. Slowly at first and hesitantly, frequently interrupted by her own sobs. By their fifth round of vodkas she had told him the whole story, her tears had given way to sniffles, and his handkerchief was a wet ball in her hand. When she looked at him with pitifully tear-swollen eyes, which were getting glassy, and asked for another drink, he couldn't refuse.

"Of course, Tillangel!"

"Don't call me that!"

"I'm sorry. Please forgive me," he said. But it was too late; he had triggered a new flow of tears. It took another drink to calm her down again.

She apologized then for weeping so much, and he noticed that she slurred her words and was very drunk.

214

"That's what friends are for, aren't they?" he assured her, beginning to feel the effect of the alcohol himself. He knew he had to be drunk when he heard himself say, "I love you, Tilla, have loved you from the start. This is the wrong moment, but maybe one day? I'll always be there for you, Tilla!" His glasses fogged up. He, too, was crying.

"Got a mop, Mack?" someone at the bar said. "One of your booths is being flooded." Arnie heard it but didn't care, for Tilla had put her arm around him. But then she excused herself to go to the bathroom. He watched her waver, take one, two uncertain steps, and lose her balance. He caught her and, his own legs somewhat unsteady, walked her to the ladies' room and anxiously waited until she came out.

"Better take you home, kid. Hold on here while I pay. Can you make it?" She nodded as he propped her against the wall, like a doll.

"Doesn't look like you're going to get a night of bliss with that one, my friend!" Mack said. Arnie couldn't reply because he had to rescue Tilla, who was slowly sinking downward. *Good old Uncle Arnie*, he thought as he lifted her. *Protector of the lovelorn. Always the gentleman. Instead of taking the errant child to your cave and ravishing her, you're going to take a long trip to Hermsdorf and deliver her home drunk but unharmed.*

They staggered to the station and into the train, where Tilla collapsed against him. He didn't move a muscle until they arrived and he had to wake her up.

215

He had meant to leave her at the door without confronting the aunt; but somehow, his legs refused to perform, and he was still standing there, Tilla on his arm, when Elizabeth opened the door. He had no choice but to introduce himself. "Arnold Steingasser," he said with a bow.

Elizabeth couldn't believe her eyes. "Where have you been? What in God's name happened?" she almost shrieked. Tilla shook herself and then fell stiffly into the apartment. "My God!" Elizabeth gasped.

"She'll be awright," Arnie said, pulling Tilla up. "Juss drunk."

"Drunk! It can't be! I'd better call a doctor. Don't you think I should call a doctor?" she asked, wringing her hands.

"Nawnaw," he assured her. "Let 'er sleep it off. Scuseme, madam." He carefully eased Tilla into a sitting position, took his arms out from under hers, and with another "Scuseme" staggered past Elizabeth out of the apartment.

Elizabeth was beside herself, but her niece wasn't answering any of her frantic questions and was oblivious to her remonstrances as well. She had no choice but to try to get her to bed, which she finally did. Before turning off the light, she tried once more. "Tilla! Tilla!" she cried. "Where have you been? Rolf was here looking for you!"

"Rolf," Tilla mumbled as she turned her head into the pillow. Elizabeth waited, but Tilla had fallen asleep.

33 Ida gave him a hearty welcoming hug, then stepped back and frowned. "You're a little pale around the edges, Rolf, my boy . . . and carrying quite a banner!"

"A banner?"

"The smell of alcohol precedes you from here to there." She held her hand at arm's length from her mouth. "Drinking in the middle of the day now, are you?"

"Must be from last night."

"Early morning sounds more likely," she said. "You know that you're skinnier than when Max first brought you here. That's over a year and a half ago." She turned him toward the window. "I don't like the looks of you."

"That's too bad," Rolf said. "I don't have any others."

Ida grimaced and slapped him on the rear. "God!" She exclaimed. "What do you sit on? Even your ass is nothing but bones. Can't you eat a little more? *Ach!* What's the point? You don't pay attention."

"Max home?"

"Can't you hear him?"

"What's he up to now?"

"Lighters. He's bought a couple truckloads of ammunition, empty machine-gun shells, I think they are. He's turning them into lighters."

"First he turns steel helmets into cooking pots"—Rolf laughed—"then it's stoves and pipes, and now lighters. What next?"

"Who knows? He thinks of something new every day, but you got to admit, whatever he comes up with, he always makes it work!" she said with pride.

"Soon you'll be Ida, the industrialist's wife."

"You think you're kidding? That's what he wants. You'll stay for dinner, won't you? I've got a meat loaf in the oven."

"I'd love to, but I'm on at six. Thank you anyway." He gave her a big, smacking, affectionate kiss and slipped something into her apron pocket, then walked through the garden to the garage.

What can you do with him? Ida asked herself as she pulled the Hershey bar from her pocket. *If only he'd take better care of himself.*

Rolf knocked on the door and when he heard the grunted "Ha?" went inside. As familiar as he was with the place, it still astonished him that Max could get work done in this unbelievable clutter, that he could, often with only a kerosene lantern for light, produce ingenious, workable things in this mess. At the moment the district had electricity. Max stood under a single lamp in baggy, dirty overalls, adjusting a vise. Rolf stepped carefully over stacks of ammunition boxes, picked his way through a maze of stacked sheet metal, bundles of aluminum stock, rusty pails filled with bolts and nuts, shoe cartons overflowing with nails and screws. He maneuvered past oil drums, spirals of wire, crates with metal shavings, table saws, band saws, all kinds of small and large machinery, squeezed himself

218

past a huge drill press, and, after almost tripping over a pile of brittle, moldy leather belts, finally stood before Max. "How's it going?"

"New life blooms in ruins! Onward and upward! Rebuilding has begun!" Max announced cheerfully, wiping his hands on the sides of his overalls and scratching his gray, unruly hair. He smiled at Rolf. "Look at our Ruff, the American! Quite a jacket you got there!" he said, feeling the fabric.

"It's got thousands of pockets," Rolf said, pleased. "Here and here—and see, another two on the inside." He showed each one in rapid succession. "It's an American army jacket. They call it an Eisenhower jacket. It's great, isn't it?"

"Sure is."

"Did you get it?" Rolf asked. Max nodded, handing him a camera. "Nice!" Rolf said. "How much?"

"Two cartons."

"One and a half."

"If that's supposed to be funny, I'm not laughing. It's a Leica II-F. There's nothing better. If your contact doesn't want to fork over two lousy cartons, tell 'im to go to hell. It's robbery as it is."

"One and a half!" Rolf repeated, grinning, and aimed the camera at Max. "Smile!"

"Careful, now!" Max admonished. "First gimme the goods; then you can fool around with it."

Rolf put the camera down, reached into his jacket, and put a carton of Chesterfields on the bench. Max, beckoning with his index finger, watched silently as five more packets appeared from Rolf's various pockets. "I said two!" Max looked impatiently at Rolf. "Come on! I don't have time for games."

Rolf, still grinning, added the other five, one by one. He picked up one of the lighters, flicked it. "Dandy." By the time his eyes returned to Max cartons and single packs had disappeared. He gestured to the rows of empty shells. "Looks like mass production already."

"It will be—eventually," Max said. "Could have been much sooner if the Russkis hadn't cleaned us out like a Christmas goose. Can't do much without tools and machinery. Why do you think they kept the Western Allies away so long? Gave them time to take away every last useful thing from cows, generators, typewriters, stoves to desks. They've even dismantled the railroad tracks. Lotta good it'll do them. They'll rot and rust because their gauge is much wider than ours. But they've shipped them to Mother Russia, along with everything else . . . including our scientists, those they could find. Can't hardly blame 'em, except they should've unscrewed things. But these maniacs were in such a hurry they used crowbars on what they couldn't yank out. Lotta stuff got ruined, won't do 'em any good."

"They overlooked a few things, didn't they?" Rolf laughed, making a sweeping gesture over the place. "Looks to me you got enough stuff here to open a factory."

"Bah!" Max snorted. "This here? A pittance! Primitive, outdated stuff. Grant you, it's better than nothin'. You gotta start somewhere. But believe me, it's no more than fills a hollow tooth. As for the factory, I'm sure as hell gonna have one. You wanna take bets on it? Man's gotta think ahead, Ruff! Lemme tell you somethin'! There's gonna be a money reform. Has to come, as sure as the 'amen' in church. And the moment money is worth somethin' again, the bottom of the black market is gonna fall out, Ruff, my boy. Then people will wanna work again, 'cause they'll be able to make a *living*. You know what a carton of cigarettes is gonna be worth?" Max paused, the better to emphasize his words. "It's gonna be worth two hundred cigarettes, Ruff. That's all. No bread, no butter, no Leica. It'll be worth exactly what it is. Two hundred coffin nails, and everyone's gonna be able to buy 'em, 'cause they'll be a pfennig apiece, or somethin' like it. Will you be ready, Ruff?"

"Ready?"

"You know what I mean! Will you have learned enough to make an honest living?"

"I don't make an honest living?" Rolf said with mock indignation. "I'm a bar pianist, playing for a fee. That's not honest?" he added seriously.

"Whatta you make?" Max said impatiently. "A hundred, two hundred a week? Not enough to buy a loaf of bread, and you know it. Wanna bet you got a couple o' thou on you right now? . . . And not from tickling the keys either."

Rolf smiled as he pulled a fat bundle of bills from one of his pockets. "Need some?"

"I knew it. Didn't I tell you?" Max said without enthusiasm. "Black-market dough. Fine as far as it goes. Enjoy it while it lasts. What I'm talking about is: What are you gonna do when it stops? You gonna go on tinkling keys every night for the amusement of ladies and gentlemen, then have a few with your pals 'cause you're too wound up to go to bed, then hit the sack until it's time to go on again . . . is that what you gonna do with your life?"

"Father Max! The voice of reason and morality!" Rolf quipped, lighting a cigarette.

"Would not do you any harm to pay attention to Father Max. You know Ida and I think of you as our son, the one we never had. Pay attention, Ruff, buddy. Bar pianists are a dime a dozen. I've seen a goodly number in my time. You gonna join the crowd of pale-faced, burned-out walking ghosts, man? You already look like something dragged out from under a stone. What's happened to the great pianist you were gonna be—ha? Don't tell me it's just gonna happen 'cause it won't, man. Never does. Nothin' comes from nothin', Ruff! You still going to the concertery or whatever it's called?"

"Yes. I'm putting in my appearances at the conservatory."

"Appearances ain't good enough, are they?"

"No."

"Then do something about it. Look at that girl! Working very hard, she is . . . and studies, from what I hear. You ain't seeing much of her, are you?" Rolf looked away and shook his head. "Well," said Max, "it's none of my business." He busied himself with one of the lighters, flipping the little wheel until, on the third try, a large blue flame sprang up. "Not bad, ha? Not bad at all. Want it? Catch!" Rolf caught it, tried it. It worked.

"Thank you!" He caressed the lighter, making sure Max watched. "I hereby christen you Max the flamethrower. Applause, please."

"See if you can get me some flints, as many as you can get your hands on."

"I'll see what I can do." Rolf hung the camera around his neck, then carefully hid it under his jacket. "I've got more customers for Leicas, Rolleis, too."

"I know. Guess you're off, ha? Can't stay for dinner?"

"No. Sorry. Got to go on at six."

"Well, we'll be seein' you." When Rolf reached the door, he called after him, "You do some thinking, Ruff."

Rolf whistled softly as he walked away. *Why didn't I tell him?* he thought, feeling guilty now. *Why didn't I tell him that I haven't seen the inside of the Bathtub in months, that I've been practicing eight, ten hours each day and catching up on composition and all the other stuff? Well, the surprise, when I hand him the tickets to my concert, will be all the greater,* he thought, soothing his conscience. *Last night and tonight, my first time off in ages.* But he felt tired, and he suddenly resented the fact that he had committed himself to play even one night at the Bathtub.

34 The day was extraordinarily warm for the end of October. All the windows in the classroom were open. From the conservatory next door, high-pitched sounds of someone practicing the flute drifted over. There were footsteps in the hallway. Professor Stephanoff and a tall, elegant gentleman came into view. They stopped just outside the open door.

"That was an experience," Stephanoff said. "The brilliant interplay of contrasting tutti and soli in this piece gets me every time. And," he continued, "it's like an incessant dialogue between the two. That's what gives the first movement its particular quality. He did it right. Ah! What a pleasure to hear it played the way it should be."

"He's one of the rare ones," the tall man said. "You can teach all your life and never get one like that. Extraordinary depth for his age."

"Age!" Stephanoff scoffed. "What's age? A lot of years in which you can become nimble-fingered and learn all the tricks. But you can't learn talent, even if you live a thousand years. The kid was born with it, just as you and I were, right, Greiner?" Both laughed and, still talking, walked down the hallway again.

Tilla had been close enough to overhear the conversation. She looked at the model, a sour-faced, nude, flabby-fleshed woman, and thought of Stephanoff. She had seen him often enough with this man to know that they were friends. But until this moment she had not known that he was Greiner, Rolf's professor. She had no doubt now that the talent mentioned was Rolf. Everything, everyone seemed to be conspiring to remind her of Rolf. It never failed to send her into a tailspin. Stephanoff was back in class, stalked once around the room, looking over everyone's shoulder, and now stood behind her. Stood there for what seemed an eternity. Suddenly, abruptly, he stepped around her easel, glared at her, and screamed, "SHIT! ABOMINABLE SHIT! LITTLE SHIT AT THAT! CHICKENSHIT!" With one quick motion he tore her drawing off the pad, crunched it into a ball, and threw it across the room. It landed next to the model's toe. "WHATEVER MADE ME ACCEPT YOU? WHAT IN THE WORLD MADE YOU THINK YOU COULD BE AN ARTIST? AREN'T THERE ENOUGH DECENT PROFESSIONS? WHY DON'T YOU BECOME A SEAMSTRESS, NURSE . . . WHAT DO I KNOW—ANYTHING! WHAT THE FUCK ARE YOU DOING IN MY CLASS?" He wheeled around and swept his hand over the assembled class. "THAT GOES FOR ALMOST EVERYONE HERE! YOU DON'T EVEN KNOW HOW TO HOLD A PENCIL, LET ALONE DRAW WITH ONE!" He turned back to face Tilla. "YOU'RE TOO FUCKING YOUNG TO BE HERE! YOU HAVEN'T LIVED; THEREFORE YOU KNOW NOTHING! NOTHING AT ALL!"

Tilla was petrified, unable even to avoid his eyes. Stephanoff always used abusive language, but she had never heard him like this. He accosted her again, asking, "DO YOU KNOW ANYTHING? WHO COMPOSED THE ITALIAN CONCERTO?"

Tilla choked on the answer because big, ugly tears were

225

rolling down her cheeks, and he hated that, she knew. Stephanoff yelled, "THE COMPOSER OF THE ITALIAN CONCERTO, ALSO KNOWN AS THE CONCERTO IN GUSTO ITALIANO, WAS ONE JOHANN SEBASTIAN BACH! EVER HEARD OF BACH?" She nodded feebly. "WELL, THAT'S AT LEAST SOMETHING—SHE'S HEARD OF BACH." His voice dropped to an almost-normal level as he turned and addressed the class at large. "Don't get me wrong! Tilla draws pretty pictures. You all do." Then he screamed, no, roared, "BUT THAT'S NOT ENOUGH! THERE'S MORE TO IT!" In a normal voice again: "There has never been a great artist who was dumb. Never will be. They all KNEW! Knew more than their palettes. They knew about music, literature, LIFE! Go on out and LIVE! LISTEN! OBSERVE!" He made another round, slowly this time, stopping for a brief moment behind every easel. He dragged his trademark, the yellow shawl, behind him and shook his head again and again, even at Gertrud's work.

"Stephanoff! You're really in a mood today, aren't you?" she said.

Audible silence until he yelled, "WHY THE HELL SHOULDN'T I BE WHEN ALL I SEE HERE IS SHIT! IS THAT SUPPOSED TO BE A NUDE? LOOKS LIKE A LIMP BAG OF WET FLOUR TO ME. NO ONE HERE—REPEAT, NO ONE HAS ANYTHING WORTH LOOKING AT. YOU HAVE NO EYES, NO EARS, NO SENSES! Take this line here, from shoulder to wrist over knee." He startled the model by tracing the line on her goose-pimpled flesh. "Right down to the ankle, one long, soft andante to, PRESTO-FORTE, the bony, crooked toe. Point and counterpoint!"

The tinny alarm went off, and the model reached for her robe. Professor Stephanoff, still shaking his head, stamped out, motioning with his head for Tilla to follow him. He waited halfway down the hall until she caught up with him. He put his arm around her shoulder. "I know I'm rough on you. But I'm rough on everyone. If you weren't so darned good, you wouldn't be in my class. You know that, don't you? The fact is, the others are much older, a little hardened already. They can take a mean, old bastard like me. You're still a kid, too sensitive, too vulnerable. I want you to switch to Professor Ballin. What do you think?"

Tilla, thunderstruck, didn't know what to say.

"Yell at me!" he said. "Scream! I would like that. Why don't you? You don't because you're scared of me."

"Yes."

"That's no good. Do you see what I mean?" She nodded, and he smiled. "A couple of semesters with old Ella won't do you any harm. Grow up, do some living, kid. There's no depth to your work; it can't be there. Go get laid. . . . See! You're blushing again, and I'm only talking about the facts of life. The next time you draw a rose, take a petal, caress it, put it on your tongue, inhale it, chew it, crumble one between your fingers to find out about its texture. That's what I'm talking about. You have to prick yourself with a thorn to understand its sharpness. Watch that rose for a week in all kinds of light; listen to the sound of a dropping

227

petal. Watch it shrink and wilt. Ah, Tilla!" He gave her a slap on the back. "Run along now. I'll speak to Lady Ballin."

She had taken one step when he reached out and pulled her ear. "I want to see your work from time to time. Don't you dare get frilly. Old Ella has a way of doing that to her students. But I won't let that happen to you."

35

"It's the merry month of May again. Looks as if we've made it through another winter," Elizabeth said cheerfully. "Oh, it's been such a beautiful day! But you probably never even stuck your nose out."

"No," said Tilla, and thought: *One whole year and three weeks ago I was still happy, and then he destroyed it all.*

"It wouldn't hurt you to smile once in a while," Elizabeth remarked.

"I want to show you something," Tilla said, eager to avoid a lecture on her disposition. She put her drawing pad on the kitchen table and propped it against the wall.

"That's Edwina!" Elizabeth exclaimed. "Amazing how you can do that. It looks just like her. She certainly is a very striking-looking young woman—being so tall helps, of course. She's got legs like Marlene Dietrich."

"She's very proud of them."

"Why shouldn't she be? Edwina von Brockdorf," Elizabeth said with an expression of pleasure, as if she were chewing candy. "It's such a nice name. How wonderful for you to have her for a friend. How fortunate that you both are in the same class and that she lives in Hermsdorf, too. Without her, you would do nothing but work and become a total recluse. What I don't understand is that she can't seem to find a boyfriend. I mean, with her looks . . . and coming from such a fine family."

"I don't have one either."

"*You!* You scare them all away. That nice Ulrich, what was his name?"

"Herter," Tilla supplied.

"Yes. Ulrich Herter. A very nice, well-mannered young man, and you wouldn't even go to the movies with him."

"What's the point?"

"And that dark-haired young doctor who brought me roses. He was so in love with you he would have kissed the ground you walked on."

"He was so boring."

"And Klaus Bauer, was he boring, too? Surely you can't be serious."

"I don't mean they were boring. It's just that I wasn't interested, I guess."

"No one's good enough for you? You'll be eighteen this October. What do you want, Tilla? If it's still that Rolf Severin, I'm afraid you've missed the boat. I can't say I blame him, and you can't accuse him of not trying! *My God!* For weeks and weeks he wrote you a letter every day.

229

Every day! I've never heard of such a thing, and you wouldn't even open them. How often did he come here? Ten, fifteen times, and not once, not once did you see him. There's a limit, Tilla, to how much a man can try. You've had your chance, but apparently you didn't want him either. I don't know what you want. Honest, I don't. All I know is that you should show common courtesy and go to his first concert. He sent us the tickets, and all you have to do is show up. That's not asking too much, considering that he used to be your great love. There was a time when all I ever heard was 'Rolf, Rolf, Rolf.' " When Tilla didn't say anything, Elizabeth said angrily, "If you don't go, it will put me in a very awkward position with the major, who has agreed to accompany us." The doorbell rang.

"That must be Weena."

"It's spring again—and birds, on the wing again," Edwina von Brockdorf sang as she danced into the kitchen. "Good evening, Mrs. Hoffart. Hi, Tilla."

"Good evening Miss von Brockdorf," Elizabeth answered. "It's certainly nice to see someone in good spirits."

"Do you like it?" Edwina asked, pointing to the drawing of herself. "At last my beautiful legs have been immortalized. They are beautiful, I must admit." She giggled, lifting her skirt high enough to reveal them in their totality. Ignoring Elizabeth's disapproving glance, she announced, "Tilla, we're going to a party tomorrow night."

"What kind of party? Where?" Tilla asked without enthusiasm.

"At Manny's. Jolly fellow," Weena explained to Elizabeth. "Kurt Mandelbaum, American born in Germany, emigrated to the States in 1936. He's some kind of big wheel in the American High Command, which is of interest only insofar as we'll get a ride home, instead of having to sit in those dreary trains . . . and equally important, there's always plenty of good food and drink, no coupons necessary, and *music!* Tilla, you'll have to see his record collection, all the great jazz from year one on. You've met him. Isn't he nice?"

Tilla only grunted and asked, "Who's coming?"

"Crowds. No, I don't know. Lots of people. Fritz, the photographer, with the Hockert antique."

"Hockert antique?"

"That's Fritz's girl friend." Weena laughed. "Her last name is Hockert, and she owns an antique shop. Clear? Karl-Kurt will probably be there, with at least two models on each arm. Oh, I can't stand that conceited ass with the 'golden voice,' " Weena said with passion.

"Is that Karl-Kurt Kremer, the radio announcer?" Elizabeth asked, impressed.

"The same," Weena answered. "He'll find his way blindfolded to wherever free drinks are served—which reminds me of Klaus and Helga Markert. Ah, well, as I said, there'll be lots of people, including assorted artists, students, actors, and, I hope, a few handsome Americans. Manny and I are going to pick you up at Dahlem Station, Tilla. Six o'clock, all right? I've promised to help him set everything up, so I

231

won't be in class tomorrow afternoon. You'll come up with something interesting for me, I'm sure, to pacify good old Ella."

"I'm not sure I want to go, and I still have that one article to illustrate," Tilla said.

"Don't pull that one on me," Weena protested. "You have till the end of next week to do it. We've spent enough weekends alone, being bored. Let's have some fun for a change."

"Why can't you go alone? I'm really not in the mood."

"You're never in the mood anymore. You were bad enough when I met you, but you're getting worse. You're no fun to be with anymore. If you don't come with me to this party, I swear I'll never talk to you again."

The combined forces of Elizabeth and Weena were too much. Tilla gave in.

It was ten past six on the big station clock when Tilla came out of the subway. The poster had been there, too. Impossible to get away from it.

PIANO RECITAL
Rolf Andreas Severin
Saturday, May 24, 1947

That would be, could have been our wedding day. She looked around for Weena, then was surprised to see Arnie.

"I'm the welcoming committee, dear Tilla. Weena is going to meet us at Flip's."

"I don't want to go there."

"Why not? It's a nice apartment, and I promise that you'll love his mother," he said, taking her arm. She took it away under the pretext of searching for something in her bag. He gave her a quick, sidelong glance but made no attempt to get close again, apparently satisfied that she was walking along without making a fuss.

"Flip is picking up his latest," he told her. "Wait till you see *this* one. A real beauty. Looks good enough to be in *Vogue*. She's modeling very cheap stuff. I guess she's just too dumb, can't eat with fork and knife, burps anytime, anywhere. Unbelievable creature. Some old geezer buys her dinner, and she goes to bed with him. It's the thing to do, she told Flip. It's a form of pride, I suppose. Proper payment for a decent meal, keeps one honest—things in balance, you know. She's a sweet one, though, not a mean bone in her gorgeous body." He shook his head. "Can you imagine? Dinner, dessert, and off to bed? Flip is trying to break her of the habit, at least partially."

"If she likes decent dinners," Tilla said, "Flip is hardly the one to provide them. He has no money."

"Doesn't have to. She takes him out."

"And as payment, he screws her—right?"

"Correct."

"That's not very nice."

"*Nice?* Kid, what's nice? The world isn't nice, don't you know that yet? It wasn't nice of that Russian grenade to run against my old man, was it? Only a couple of bloody pieces left of him, not enough to ship home. And it wasn't nice of that bomb to fall on our house, especially while my mother and sisters were still in it. You'll have to admit that wasn't nice. And the piece of shrapnel I still have in my hide isn't nice either."

"I'm . . . I didn't know . . . I didn't mean—"

"It's all right, kid. Forget it," he said, interrupting her. "Just don't talk about nice and being nice to Uncle Arnie."

"But you were nice to me."

"Accident. Pure accident. Only proves the rule. Forget the word 'nice' exists. You'll be better off."

"But, Arnie, there has to be something, some code. If one can't even be ni—I mean, decent to one's friends, what's left?"

"Decent to one's friends?" he scoffed. "You sure as hell don't know what that means, so how the hell . . ."

They walked in silence for a while until he broke it. "The one time this bum Flip has a job, emcees a fashion show, he finds himself this jewel. Why doesn't something like that ever happen to me? You won't even walk arm in arm with me. I'm good, trusty Uncle Arnie, comfortable like an old shoe. Why can't you love me, Tilla? No! Don't answer. I know it's no go. Forget what I said, and anyway, here we are." He knocked, and the door was opened immediately by a small, prim-looking elderly woman.

"Arnold!" she reprimanded him. "We *do* have a bell. How often do I have to tell you that? We are not tenement dwellers."

"You're not supposed to get excited, Mother Peters," Arnie said, patting her on the shoulder. "This is Tilla Wenkenberg. She's an art student."

234

Thin-lipped smile, as she eyed Tilla suspiciously. "Philip has told me about you. You are a very talented young lady then?"

"Mother Peters!" Arnie answered for her. "Don't you know that we only have talented friends?" He let himself fall into one of the deep leather chairs, and Mother Peters, still standing, obviously disapproved.

A key turned in the lock, and Flip entered with a tall blonde. He bowed with a grand, theatrical gesture and announced, "Ladies and gentlemen, may I have your attention! I would like to introduce you to the incomparable, singularly beautiful Miss Barbara Schmitt."

"Tahtahratah!" Arnie hooted in imitation of a trumpet.

"Barbara Schmitt, henceforth to be known, in this illustrious circle, as Schmitten." Flip nudged her. "Make your curtsies, dear; then shake hands with Mother, the revered Frau Dr. Peters, widow of the honorable but unfortunately deceased Dr. Franz Paul Peters."

Schmitten actually did a curtsy, reaping, for her effort, a sour smile from Frau Dr. Peters.

"Now, dearie," Flip ordered, "shake hands with Tilla, a misguided child, who insists on studying art, instead of marrying fame and fortune," he said, with a meaningful glance at Tilla. "Another flower of German womanhood wasted!"

Schmitten and Tilla shook hands. "It must be very interesting to study art?" she said in a high, squeaky voice. Tilla only nodded because she was too overwhelmed by the physical beauty of this girl. Flip turned Schmitten toward Arnie.

"Give this not-so-honorable gentleman, Esquire Arnold the Steingasser, a kiss dear. *Un baiser,* as we say in French or if you prefer the Viennese way, a *busserl."*

"Oh, cut the crap!" Arnie said, grabbing Schmitten around the waist and planting her on his lap, where she settled herself comfortably.

Tilla marveled at the peach skin, the heavy, honest-to-goodness blond hair, the blue-green eyes, and the figure. A high, round bosom, neither too much nor too little. Everything about Schmitten was perfect, including the extra-long, shapely legs. Schmitten on Arnie's lap absent-mindedly curled strands of his hair over her finger. *Is she unaware that he is feeling her breast,* Tilla wondered, *or doesn't she care?*

"Aren't they perfect?" Flip asked, cupping Schmitten's other breast, as someone pounded on the door.

Flip opened it, and Weena burst in. "Come on, everybody, let's go!"

They were the first guests and remained the only ones until Fritz and the Hockert antique arrived. Karl-Kurt made an entrance, introduced his fiancée, Birgit. Birgit surveyed the scene and must have found it wanting, for she and Karl-Kurt left shortly afterward. No one else showed up. It wasn't a party, and Tilla thought, *I could have told her so.* She knew Weena was disappointed. Tilla couldn't care less. She had taken refuge in the dark corner by the records, sat there feeling utterly lonely and unbearably miserable. Weena sought her out to complain, "The way they all crowd around her, you'd think they were stranded on an island and she was the only female." She was referring to Schmitten.

At ten o'clock they were still only eight, and to judge by the mountain of sandwiches Manny and Weena had prepared, he had expected at least twenty. Tilla was wondering how to get Weena to come home with her when she heard her say to Manny, "Everyone's falling asleep, Manny! Can't you put on some peppy music?"

"I have a better idea," he replied. "Let's all go to the Bathtub!" It got an instantaneous, enthusiastic reaction from everyone. Five minutes later they were in the cars. Weena, Arnie, and Tilla in Manny's, Flip and Schmitten with Fritz and Hockert.

"Please, Manny!" Tilla begged quietly. "Let me out at the first station. I'll take the train home."

"You're coming along!" Weena screamed. "I'm sick of your theatrics!"

"You call it theatrics when I want to go home?"

"You're not going to spoil my evening!"

They had fought, and when Manny stopped the car, they were at the Bathtub. Tilla wanted to run, but they wouldn't let her, pleading, arguing, pulling. She gave up only when they started shouting in chorus, "TIL-LA SPOILSPORT! SPOIL-SPORT TIL-LA!"

Their group of eight elbowed their way in the dark to a corner table Manny had managed to get. They took their seats to the last strands of "Sentimental Journey." *Dah-dah-*

dah, went the piano. The stage remained dark. *Dah-dah-dah*, there it was. The spotlight was on the piano. Tilla knew without looking up it was Rolf. Rolf played and sang "the song."

It took all her strength to suppress the sob choking her. She got up, stumbled through those standing around to the nearby ladies' room, closed the door with meticulous care to be quiet, and, holding onto the sink, allowed herself to dissolve in tears. The applause outside sounded like distant thunder. Now was the moment to escape. The lights were still out as she made her way, crouching, to the exit, stumbled through the door. Took one step, let herself fall against the wall of the building, clawed at it, sobbing.

"What more do you want, Tilla? He loves you! Go to him, make up!" It was Arnie's voice behind her.

"I can't. Not after what he's done!"

"You dumb broad!" Arnie sounded mean, angry when she expected sympathy. "Are you really, seriously going to hold one lousy screw against him for the rest of your life? I'll tell you something, Tilla, and you'd better listen! If you can't forgive, he's better off without you. You're one cold-blooded bitch. I told you I love you, and God knows I do, but it was my one lucky day, the best thing in my life, that you didn't fall in love with me.

"What is it with you? Pride? You can go and stuff it, Miss Tilla. Who the hell do you think you are? That was some performance. You were splendid. Be proud of yourself. I lose a bet. Do you know there are bets out, on how long you two can keep it up?

"Bets?"

"Yeah, bets! Ever heard of odds? The odds are ten to one that Rolf will regain his sanity and forget that you ever existed. Bets to be paid tomorrow night."

"No!" she wailed and, sobbing, clung to him.

Arnie shook her. "Maybe you're just waiting for tomorrow night—maximum effect!"

"No! No, no. I love him!"

"Then why the hell, you stupid, stubborn girl, don't you go in, talk to him, and set things straight? Will you or won't you?"

"Yes."

"Yes what? Let me hear you say it!"

"I will . . . *I want him!* I—" She first saw the shadow in the dim light of the entrance, then a dark figure, the one she could have picked out among millions. He came slowly toward her, one step at a time. She let go of Arnie, ran to him with open arms. "Rolf! Rolf! Rolf!"

"Tilla," he said softly, "my Tillangel," as his arms enfolded her.

The atmosphere was charged with happy, expectant energy; it flowed like a current through the audience—a large audience. There wasn't an empty seat in the house. Everyone was there. Jan and Kovack, Harald, Schmitten between Arnie and Flip. Professor Ella Ballin in basic black with pearls. Mary and Colonel Schenke, Jerry next to them. Stephanoff, easily visible by virtue of his yellow shawl. Max with bow tie dressed in, as he told Elizabeth, a tailor-made midnight blue suit, the absolute best! Ida, carefully coiffed, at his side. Edith Severin . . .

"Look at Mrs. Severin," Elizabeth whispered into Tilla's ear. "How can she possibly wear something like that . . . and her son is performing!"

Edith, true enough, wore a dress with an astonishingly large floral pattern, which seemed to spill over on small white-haired Professor Seewald.

"Is that his mother?" Weena said from behind her as the lights dimmed and Rolf appeared onstage.

"That's my buddy up there!" Max said loud enough to be heard over the applause.

Elizabeth said, *"Psst!"* at the same time as she took Major Duncan Macdonnell's hand off her knee.

ILSE KOEHN was born in Berlin, Germany. She studied graphic design and illustration at the Hochschule fuer Bildende Kuenste in her native city and later worked as a free-lance writer and illustrator for various magazines. She was first-prize winner in a national soap poster contest (the poster was then displayed thoughout Germany) and designed exhibits for industrial fairs.

She came to the United States in 1958 and has worked as art director for both the J. Walter Thompson Co. and the Campbell-Downe Advertising Agency. Ms. Koehn has exhibited her paintings at the Lynn Kottler Galleries and in private collections. Since 1968 she has been a free-lance book illustrator and designer. She now lives in Connecticut with her husband John Van Zwienen, also a graphic artist and writer.

Ilse Koehn is the author of the prize-winning *Mischling, Second Degree: My Childhood in Nazi Germany*. *Tilla* is her first novel.